The Secret of the Tower

The Secret of the Tower

Anthony Hope

WAKING LION PRESS

ISBN 1-60096-505-9

Published by Waking Lion Press, an imprint of The Editorium

Waking Lion Press™, the Waking Lion Press logo, and The Editorium™ are trademarks of The Editorium, LLC

The Editorium, LLC
West Valley City, UT 84128-3917
wakinglionpress.com
wakinglion@editorium.com

Contents

Contents

Chapter 1

Doctor Mary's Paying Guest

"Just in time, wasn't it?" asked Mary Arkroyd.

"Two days before the—the ceremony! Mercifully it had all been kept very quiet, because it was only three months since poor Gilly was killed. I forget whether you ever met Gilly? My half-brother, you know?"

"Only once—in Collingham Gardens. He had an *exeat,* and dashed in one Saturday morning when we were just finishing our work. Don't you remember?"

"Yes, I think I do. But since my engagement I'd gone into colors. Oh, of course I've gone back into mourning now! And everything was ready—settlements and so on, you know. And rooms taken at Bournemouth. And then it all came out!"

"How?"

"Well, Eustace—Captain Cranster, I mean. Oh, I think he really must have had shell-shock, as he said, even though the doctor seemed to doubt it! He gave the Colonel as a reference in some shop, and—and the bank wouldn't pay the check. Other checks turned up, too, and in the end the police went through his papers, and found letters from—well, from her, you know. From Bogota. South America, isn't it? He'd lived there ten years, you know, growing something—beans, or coffee, or coffee-beans, or something—I don't know what. He tried to say the marriage wasn't binding, but the Colonel—wasn't it providential that the Colonel was home on leave? Mamma could never have grappled with it! The Colonel was sure it was, and so were the lawyers."

"What happened then?"

"The great thing was to keep it quiet. Now, wasn't it? And there was the shell-shock—or so Eustace—Captain Cranster, I mean—said, anyhow. So, on the Colonel's advice, Mamma squared the check business and—and they gave him twenty-four hours to clear out. Papa—I call the Colonel Papa, you know, though he's really my stepfather—used a little influence, I think. Anyhow it was managed. I never saw him again, Mary."

"Poor dear! Was it very bad?"

"Yes! But—suppose we had been married! Mary, where should I have been?"

Mary Arkroyd left that problem alone. "Were you very fond of him?" she asked.

"Awfully!" Cynthia turned up to her friend pretty blue eyes suffused in tears. "It was the end of the world to me. That there could be such men! I went to bed. Mamma could do nothing with me. Oh, well, she wrote to you about all that."

"She told me you were in a pretty bad way."

"I was just desperate! Then one day—in bed—the thought of you came. It seemed an absolute inspiration. I remembered the card you sent on my last birthday—you've never forgotten my birthdays, though it's years since we met—with your new address here—and your 'Doctor,' and all the letters after your name! I thought it rather funny." A faint smile, the first since Miss Walford's arrival at Inkston, probably the first since Captain Eustace Cranster's shell-shock had wrought catastrophe—appeared on her lips. "How I waited for your answer! You don't mind having me, do you, dear? Mamma insisted on suggesting the P.G. arrangement. I was afraid you'd shy at it."

"Not a bit! I should have liked to have you anyhow, but I can make you much more comfortable with the P.G. money. And your maid too—she looks as if she was accustomed to the best! By the way, need she be quite so tearful? She's more tearful than you are yourself."

"Jeanne's very, very fond of me," Cynthia murmured reproachfully.

"Oh, well get her out of that," said Mary briskly. "The tears, I mean, not the fondness. I'm very fond of you myself. Six years ago you were a charming kitten, and I used to enjoy being your 'visiting governess'—to say nothing of finding the guineas very handy while I was waiting to qualify. You're rather like a kitten still, one of those blue-eyed ones—Siamese, aren't they?—with close fur and a wondering look. But you mustn't mew down here, and you must have lots of milk and cream. Even if rations go on, I can certify all the extras for you. That's the good of being a doctor!" She laughed cheerfully as she took a cigarette from the mantelpiece and lit it.

Cynthia, on the other hand, began to sob prettily and not in a noisy fashion, yet evidently heading towards a bout of grief. Moreover, no sooner had the first sound of lamentation escaped from her lips, than the door was opened smartly and a buxom girl, in lady's maid uniform, rushed in, darted across the room, and knelt by Cynthia, sobbing also and exclaiming, "Oh, my poor Mees Cynthia!"

Mary smiled in a humorous contempt.

"Stop this!" she commanded rather brusquely. "You've not been deceived too, have you, Jeanne?"

"Me, madame? No. My poor Mees—"

"Leave your poor Mees to me." She took a paper bag from the mantelpiece. "Go and eat chocolates."

Fixed with a firm and decidedly professional glance, Jeanne stopped sobbing and rose slowly to her feet.

"Don't listen outside the door. You must have been listening. Wait till you're rung for. Miss Cynthia will be all right with me. We're going for a walk. Take her upstairs and put her hat on her, and a thick coat; it's cold and going to rain, I think."

"A walk, Mary?" Cynthia's sobs stopped, to make way for this protest. The description of the weather did not sound attractive.

"Yes, yes. Now off with both of you! Here, take the chocolates, Jeanne, and try to remember that it might have been worse."

Jeanne's brown eyes were eloquent of reproach.

"Captain Cranster might have been found out too late—after the wedding," Mary explained with a smile. "Try to look at it like that. Five minutes to get ready, Cynthia!" She was ready for the weather herself, in the stout coat and skirt and weather-proof hat in which she had driven the two-seater on her round that morning.

The disconsolate pair drifted ruefully from the room, though Jeanne did recollect to take the chocolates. Doctor Mary stood looking down at the fire, her lips still shaped in that firm, wise, and philosophical smile with which doctors and nurses—and indeed, sometimes, anybody who happens to be feeling pretty well himself—console, or exasperate, suffering humanity. "A very good thing the poor silly child did come to me!" That was the form her thoughts took. For although Dr. Mary Arkroyd was, and knew herself to be, no dazzling genius at her profession—in moments of candor she would speak of having "scraped through" her qualifying examinations—she had a high opinion of her own common sense and her power of guiding weaker mortals.

For all that Jeanne's cheek bulged with a chocolate, there was open resentment on her full, pouting lips, and a hint of the same feeling in Cynthia's still liquid eyes, when mistress and maid came downstairs again. Without heeding these signs, Mary drew on her gauntlets, took her walking-stick, and flung the hall door open. A rush of cold wind filled the little hall. Jeanne shivered ostentatiously; Cynthia sighed and muffled herself deeper in her fur collar. "A good walking day!" said Mary decisively.

Up to now, Inkston had not impressed Cynthia Walford very favorably. It was indeed a mixed kind of a place. Like many villages which lie near to London and have been made, by modern developments, more accessible than once they were, it showed chronological strata in its buildings. Down by the station all was new, red, suburban. Mounting the tarred road, the wayfarer bore slightly to the right along the original village street; bating the aggressive "fronts" of one or two commercial innovators, this was old, calm, serene, gray in tone and restful, ornamented by three or four good class Georgian houses, one quite fine, with well wrought iron gates (this was Dr. Irechester's); turning to the right again, but more sharply, the wayfarer found himself once more in villadom, but a villadom more ornate, more costly, with gardens to be measured in acres—or nearly. This was Hinton Avenue (Hinton because it was the maiden name of the builder's wife; Avenue because avenue is genteel). Here Mary dwelt, but by good luck her predecessor, Dr. Christian Evans, had seized upon a surviving old cottage at the end of the avenue, and, indeed, of Inkston village itself. Beyond it stretched meadows, while the road, turning again, ran across an open heath, and pursued its way to Sprotsfield, four miles distant, a place of greater size where all amenities could be found.

It was along this road that the friends now walked, Mary setting a brisk pace. "When once you've turned your back on the Avenue, it's heaps better," she said. "Might be real country, looking this way, mightn't it? Except the Naylors' place—Oh, and Tower Cottage—there are no houses between this and Sprotsfield."

The wind blew shrewdly, with an occasional spatter of rain; the withered bracken lay like a vast carpet of dull copper-color under the cloudy sky; scattered fir-trees made fantastic shapes in the early gloom of a December day. A somber scene, yet wanting only sunshine to make it flash in a richness of color; even to-day its quiet and spaciousness, its melancholy and monotony, seemed to bid a sympathetic and soothing welcome to aching and fretted hearts.

"It really is rather nice out here," Cynthia admitted.

"I come almost every afternoon. Oh, I've plenty of time! My round in the morning generally sees me through—except for emergencies, births and deaths, and so on. You see, my predecessor, poor Christian Evans, never had more than the leavings, and that's all I've got. I believe the real doctor, the old-established one, Dr. Irechester, was angry at first with Dr. Evans for coming; he didn't want a rival. But Christian was such a meek, mild, simple little Welshman, not the least pushing or ambitious; and very soon Dr. Irechester, who's quite well off, was glad to leave him the dirty work, I mean (she explained, smiling) the cottages, and the panel work, National Insurance, you know, and so on. Well, as you know, I came down as *locum* for Christian, he was a fellow-student of mine, and when the dear little man was killed in France, Dr. Irechester himself suggested that I should stay on. He was rather nice. He said, 'We all started to laugh at you, at first, but we don't laugh now, anyhow, only my wife does! So, if you stay on, I don't doubt we shall work very well together, my dear colleague,' Wasn't that rather nice of him, Cynthia?"

"Yes, dear," said Cynthia, in a voice that sounded a good many miles away.

Mary laughed. "I'm bound to be interested in you, but I suppose you're not bound to be interested in me," she observed resignedly. "All the same, I made a sensation at Inkston just at first. And they were even more astonished when it turned out that I could dance and play lawn tennis."

"That's a funny little place," said Cynthia, pointing to the left side of the road.

"Tower Cottage, that's called."

"But what a funny place!" Cynthia insisted. "A round tower, like a Martello tower, only smaller, of course; and what looks just like an ordinary cottage or small farmhouse joined on to it. What could the tower have been for?"

"I'm sure I don't know. Origin lost in the mists of antiquity! An old gentleman named Saffron lives there now."

"A patient of yours, Mary?"

"Oh, no! He's well off, rich, I believe. So he belongs to Dr. Irechester. But I often meet him along the road. Lately there's always been a younger man with him, a companion, or secretary, or something of that sort, I hear he is."

"There are two men coming along the road now."

"Yes, that's them, the old man, and his friend. He's rather striking to look at."

"Which of them?"

"The old man, of course. I haven't looked at the secretary. Cynthia, I believe you're beginning to feel a little better!"

"Oh, no, I'm not! I'm afraid I'm not, really!" But there had been a cheerfully roguish little smile on her face. It vanished very promptly when observed.

The two men approached them, on their way, no doubt, to Tower Cottage. The old man was not above middle height, indeed, scarcely reached it; but he made the most of his inches carrying himself very upright, with an air of high dignity. Close-cut white hair showed under an old-fashioned peaked cap; he wore a plaid shawl swathed round him, his left arm being enveloped in its folds; his right rested in the arm of his companion, who was taller than he, lean and loose-built, clad in an almost white (and very unseasonable looking) suit of some homespun material. He wore no covering on his head, a thick crop of curly hair (of a color indistinguishable in the dim light) presumably affording such protection as he needed. His face was turned down towards the old man, who was looking up at him and apparently talking to him, though in so low a tone that no sound reached Mary and Cynthia as they passed by. Neither man gave any sign of noticing their presence.

"Mr. Saffron, you said? Rather a queer name, but he looks a nice old man; patriarchal, you know. What's the name of the other one?"

"I did hear; somebody mentioned him at the Naylors'— somebody who had heard something about him in France. What was the name? It was something queer too, I think."

"They've got queer names, and they live in a queer house!" Cynthia actually gave a little laugh. "But are you going to walk all night, Mary dear?"

"Oh, poor thing! I forgot you! You're tired? We'll turn back."

They retraced their steps, again passing Tower Cottage, into which its occupants must have gone, for they were no longer to be seen.

"That name's on the tip of my tongue," said Mary in amused vexation. "I shall get it in a moment!"

Cynthia had relapsed into gloom. "It doesn't matter in the least," she murmured.

"It's Beaumaroy!" said Mary in triumph.

"I don't wonder you couldn't remember that!"

Chapter 2

The General Remembers

Amongst other various, and no doubt useful, functions, Miss Delia Wall performed that of gossip and news agent-general to the village of Inkston. A hard-featured, swarthy spinster of forty, with a roving, inquisitive, yet not un-kindly eye, she perambulated—or rather percycled—the district, taking stock of every incident. Not a cat could kitten or a dog have the mange without her privity; critics of her mental activity went near to insinuating connivance. Naturally, therefore, she was well acquainted with the new development at Tower Cottage, although the isolated position of that dwelling made thorough observation piquantly difficult. She laid her information before an attentive, if not very respectful, audience gathered round the tea-table at Old Place, the Naylors' handsome house on the outskirts of Sprotsfield and on the far side of the heath from Inkston. She was enjoying herself, although she was, as usual, a trifle distrustful of the quality of Mr. Naylor's smile; it smacked of the satiric. "He looks at you as if you were a specimen," she had once been heard to complain; and, when she said "specimen," it was obviously beetles that she had in mind.

"Everybody knows old Mr. Saffron—by sight, I mean—and the woman who does for him," she said. "There's never been anything remarkable about *them*. He took his walk as regular as clockwork every afternoon, and she bought just the same things every week; her books must have tallied almost to a penny every month, Mrs. Naylor! I know it! And it was a very rare thing indeed for Mr. Saffron to go to London—though I have known him to be away once or twice. But very, very rarely!" She paused and added dramatically, "Until the armistice!"

"Full of ramifications, that event, Miss Wall. It affects even my business." Mr. Naylor, though now withdrawn from an active share in its conduct, was still interested in the large shipping firm from which he had drawn his comfortable fortune.

She looked at him suspiciously, as he put the ends of the slender white fingers of his two hands together, and leant forward to listen with that smile of his and eyes faintly twinkling. But the problem was seething in her brain; she had to go on.

"A week after the armistice Mr. Saffron went to London by the 9.50. He traveled first, Anna."

"Did he, dear?" Mrs. Naylor, a stout and placid dame, was not yet stirred to excitement.

"He came down by the 4.11, and those two men with him. And they've been there ever since!"

"Two men, Delia! I've only seen one."

"Oh yes, there's another! Sergeant Hooper they call him; a short thickset man with a black mustache. He buys two bottles of rum every week at the *Green Man*. And—one minute, please, Mr. Naylor—"

"I was only going to say that it looks to me as if this man Hooper were, or had been, a soldier. What do you think?"

"Never mind, Papa! Go on, Miss Wall. I'm interested." This encouragement came from Gertie Naylor, a pretty girl of seventeen who was consuming much tea, bread, and honey.

"And since then the old gentleman and this Mr. Beaumaroy go to town regularly every week on Wednesdays! Now who are they, how did Mr. Saffron get hold of them, and what are they doing here? I'm at a loss, Anna."

Apparently an *impasse!* And Mr. Naylor did not seem to assist matters by asking whether Miss Wall had kept a constant eye on the Agony Column. Mrs. Naylor took up her knitting and switched off to another topic.

"Dr. Arkroyd's friend, Delia dear! What a charming girl she looks!"

"Friend, Anna? I didn't know that! A patient, I understand, anyhow. She's taking Valentine's beef juice. Of course they *do* give that in drink cases, but I should be sorry to think—"

"Drugs, more likely," Mr. Naylor suavely interposed. Then he rose from his chair and began to pace slowly up and down the long room, looking at his beautiful pictures, his beautiful china, his beautiful chairs, all the beautiful things that were his. His family took no notice of this roving up and down; it was a habit, and was tacitly accepted as meaning that he had, for the moment, had enough of the company, and even of his own sallies at its expense.

"I've asked Dr. Arkroyd to bring her over, Miss Walford, I mean, the first day it's fine enough for tennis," Mrs. Naylor pursued. There was a hard court at Old Place, so that winter did not stop the game entirely.

"What a name, too!"

"Walford? It's quite a good name, Delia."

"No, no, Anna! Beaumaroy, of course." Miss Wall was back at the larger problem.

"There's Alec's voice. He and the General are back from their golf. Ring for another teapot, Gertie dear!"

The door opened, not Alec, but the General came in, and closed the door carefully behind him; it was obviously an act of precaution and not merely a normal exercise of good manners. Then he walked up to his hostess and said, "It's not my fault, Anna. Alec would do it, though I shook my head at him, behind the fellow's back."

"What do you mean, General?" cried the hostess. Mr. Naylor, for his part, stopped roving.

The door again! "Come in, Mr. Beaumaroy—here's tea."

Mr. Beaumaroy obediently entered, in the wake of Captain Alec Naylor, who duly presented him to Mrs. Naylor, adding that Beaumaroy had been kind enough to make the fourth in a game with the General, the Rector of Sprotsfield, and himself. "And he and the parson were too tough a nut for us, weren't they, sir?" he added to the General.

Besides being an excellent officer and a capital fellow, Alec Naylor was also reputed to be one of the handsomest men in the Service; six foot three, very straight, very fair, with features as regular as any romantic hero of them all, and eyes as blue. The honorable limp that at present marked his movements would, it was hoped, pass away. Even his own family were often surprised into a new admiration of his physical perfections, remarking, one to the other, how Alec took the shine out of every other man in the room.

There was no shine, no external obvious shine, to take out of Mr. Beaumaroy, Miss Wall's puzzling, unaccounted-for Mr. Beaumaroy. The light showed him now more clearly than when Mary Arkroyd met him on the heath road, but perhaps thereby did him no service. His features, though irregular, were not ugly or insignificant, but he wore a rather battered aspect; there were deep lines running from the corners of his mouth, and crowsfeet had started under the gray eyes which, in their turn, looked more skeptical than ardent, rather mocking than eager. Yet when he smiled, his face became not merely pleasant, but confidentially pleasant; he seemed to smile especially to and for the person to whom he was talking; and his voice was notably agreeable, soft and clear—the voice of a high-bred man, but not exactly of a high-bred English-man. There was no accent definite enough to be called foreign, certainly not to be assigned to any particular race, but there was an exotic touch about his manner of speech suggesting that, even if not that of a foreigner, it was shaped and colored by the inflexions of foreign tongues. The hue of his plentiful and curly hair, indistinguishable to Mary and Cynthia, now stood revealed as neither black, nor red, nor auburn, nor brown, nor golden, but just, and rather surprisingly, a plain yellow, the color of a cowslip or thereabouts. Altogether rather a rum-looking fellow! This had been Alec Naylor's first remark when the Rector of Sprotsfield pointed him out, as a possible fourth, at the golf club, and the rough justice of the description could not be denied. He, like Alec, bore his scars; the little finger of his right hand was amputated down to the knuckle.

Yet, after all this description, in particularity if not otherwise worthy of a classic novelist, the thing yet remains that most struck observers. Mr. Hector Beaumaroy had an adorable candor of manner. He answered questions with innocent readiness and pellucid sincerity. It would be impossible to think him guilty of a lie; ungenerous to suspect so much as a suppression of the truth. Even Mr. Naylor, hardened by five-and-thirty years' experience of what sailors will blandly swear to in collision cases, was struck with the open candor of his bearing.

"Yes," he said. "Yes, Miss Wall, that's right, we go to town every Wednesday. No particular reason why it should be Wednesday, but old gentlemen somehow do better—don't you think so?—with method and regular habits."

"I'm sure you know what's best for Mr. Saffron," said Delia. "You've known him a long time, haven't you?"

Mr. Naylor drew a little nearer and listened. The General had put himself into the corner, a remote corner of the room, and sat there with an uneasy and rather glowering aspect.

"Oh no, no!" answered Beaumaroy. "A matter of weeks only. But the dear old fellow seemed to take to me—a friend put us in touch originally. I seem to be able to do just what he wants."

"I hope your friend is not really ill, not seriously?" This time the question was Mrs. Naylor's, not Miss Delia's.

"His health is really not so bad, but," he gave a glance round the company, as though inviting their understanding, "he insists that he's not the man he was."

"Absurd!" smiled Naylor. "Not much older than I am, is he?"

"Only just turned seventy, I believe. But the idea's very persistent."

"Hypochondria!" snapped Miss Delia.

"Not altogether. I'm afraid there is a little real heart trouble. Dr. Irechester—"

"Oh, with Dr. Irechester, dear Mr. Beaumaroy, you're all right!"

Again Beaumaroy's glance—that glance of innocent appeal—ranged over the company (except the General, out of its reach). He seemed troubled and embarrassed.

"A most accomplished man, evidently, and a friend of yours, of course. But, well, there it is, a mere fancy, of course, but unhappily my old friend doesn't take to him. He, he thinks that he's rather inquisitorial. A doctor's duty, I suppose—"

"Irechester's a sound man, a very sound man," said Mr. Naylor. "And, after all one can ask almost any question if one does it tactfully, can't one, Miss Wall?"

"As a matter of fact, he's only seen Mr. Saffron twice—he had a little chill. But his manner, unfortunately, rather, er—alarmed—"

Gertie Naylor, with the directness of youth, propounded a solution of the difficulty. "If you don't like Dr. Irechester—"

"Oh, it's not I who—"

"Why not have Mary?" Gertie made her suggestion eagerly. She was very fond of Mary, who, from the height of age, wisdom and professional dignity, had stooped to offer her an equal friendship.

"She means Dr. Mary Arkroyd," Mrs. Naylor explained.

"Yes, I know, Mrs. Naylor, I know about Dr. Arkroyd. In fact, I know her by sight. But—"

"Perhaps you don't believe in women doctors?" Alec suggested.

"It's not that. I've no prejudices. But the responsibility is on me, and I know very little of her; and, well to change one's doctor, it's rather invidious—"

"Oh, as to that, Irechester's a sensible man; he's got as much work as he wants, and as much money too. He won't resent an old man's fancy."

"Well, I'd never thought of a change, but if you all suggest it—" Somehow it did seem as if they all, and not merely youthful Gertie had suggested it. "But I should rather like to know Dr. Arkroyd first."

"Come and meet her here; that's very simple. She often comes to tennis and tea. We'll let you know the first time she's coming."

Beaumaroy most cordially accepted the idea and the invitation. "Any afternoon I shall be delighted, except Wednesdays. Wednesdays are sacred, aren't they, Miss Wall? London on Wednesdays for Mr. Saffron and me, and the old brown bag!" He laughed in a quiet merriment. "That old bag's been in a lot of places with me and has carried some queer cargoes. Now it just goes to and fro, between here and town, with Mudie books. Must have books, living so much alone as we do!" He had risen as he spoke, and approached Mrs. Naylor to take leave.

She gave him her hand very cordially. "I don't suppose Mr. Saffron cares to meet people; but any spare time you have, Mr. Beaumaroy, we shall be delighted to see you."

Beaumaroy bowed as he thanked her, adding, "And I'm promised a chance of meeting Dr. Arkroyd before long?"

The promise was renewed and the visitor took his leave, declining Alec's offer to "run him home" in the car. "The car might startle my old friend," he pleaded. Alec saw him off, and returned to find the General, who had contrived to avoid more than a distant bow of farewell to Beaumaroy, standing on the hearthrug apparently in a state of some agitation.

The envious years had refused to Major-General Punnit, C.B.—he was a distant cousin of Mrs. Naylor's—the privilege of serving his country in the Great War. His career had lain mainly in India and was mostly behind him even at the date of the South African War, in which, however, he had done valuable work in one of the supply services. He as short, stout, honest, brave, shrewd, obstinate, and as full of prejudices, religious, political and personal as an egg is of meat. And all this time he had been slowly and painfully recalling what his young friend Colonel Merman (the Colonel was young only relatively to the General) had told him about Hector Beaumaroy. The name had struck on his memory the moment the Rector pronounced it, but it had taken him a long while to "place it" accurately. However, now he had it pat; the conversation in the club came back. He retailed it now to the company at Old Place.

A pleasant fellow, Beaumaroy; socially a very agreeable fellow. And as for courage, as brave as you like. Indeed he might have had letters after his name save for the fact that he—the Colonel—would never recommend a man unless his discipline was as good as his leading, and his conduct at the base as praiseworthy as at the front. (Alec Naylor nodded his handsome head in grave approval; his father looked a little discontented, as though he were swallowing unpalatable, though wholesome, food). His whole idea—Beaumaroy's, that is—was to shield offenders, to prevent the punishment fitting the crime, even to console and countenance the wrongdoer. No sense of discipline, no moral sense, the Colonel had gone as far as that.

19

Impossible to promote or to recommend for reward, almost impossible to keep. Of course, if he had been caught young and put through the mill, it might have been different. "It *might*" the Colonel heavily underlined the possibility, but he came from Heaven knew where, after a life spent Heaven knew how. "And he seemed to know it himself," the Colonel had said, thoughtfully rolling his port round in the glass. "Whenever I wigged him, he offered to go; said he'd chuck his commission and enlist; said he'd be happier in the ranks. But I was weak, I couldn't bear to do it." After thus quoting his friend, the General added: "He was weak, damned weak, and I told him so."

"Of course he ought to have got rid of him," said Alec. "Still, sir, there's nothing, er, disgraceful."

"It seems hardly to have come to that," the General admitted reluctantly.

"It all rather makes me like him," Gertie affirmed courageously.

"I think that, on the whole, we may venture to know him in times of peace," Mr. Naylor summed up.

"That's your look out," remarked the General. "I've warned you. You can do as you like."

Delia Wall had sat silent through the story. Now she spoke up, and got back to the real point:

"There's nothing in all that to show how he comes to be at Mr. Saffron's."

The General shrugged his shoulders. "Oh, Saffron be hanged! He's not the British Army," he said.

Chapter 3

Saffron at Home

To put it plainly, Sergeant Hooper—he had been a Sergeant for a brief and precarious three weeks, but he used the title in civil life whenever he safely could, and he could at Inkston—Sergeant Hooper was a villainous-looking dog. Beaumaroy, fresh from the comely presences of Old Place, unconscious of how the General had ripped up his character and record, pleasantly nursing a little project concerning Dr. Mary Arkroyd, had never been more forcibly struck with his protege's ill-favoredness than when he arrived home on this same evening, and the Sergeant met him at the door.

"By gad, Sergeant," he observed pleasantly, "I don't think anybody could be such a rascal as you look. It's that faith that carries me through."

The Sergeant helped him off with his coat. "It's some people's stock-in-trade," he remarked, "not to look a rascal like they really are, sir." The "sir" stuck out of pure habit; it carried no real implication of respect.

"Meaning me!" laughed Beaumaroy. "How's the old man to-night?"

"Quiet enough. He's in the Tower there—been there an hour or more."

The cottage door opened on to a narrow passage, with a staircase on one side, and on the other a door leading to a small square parlor, cheerfully if cheaply furnished, and well lit by an oil lamp. A fire blazed on the hearth, and Beaumaroy sank into a "saddle-bag" armchair beside it, with a sigh of comfort. The Sergeant had jerked his head towards another door, on the right of the fireplace; it led to the Tower. Beaumaroy's eyes settled on it.

"An hour or more, has he? Have you heard anything?"

"He was making a speech a little while back, that's all."

"No more complaints and palpitations, or anything of that sort?"

"Not as I've heard. But he never says much to me. Mrs. Wiles gets the benefit of his symptoms mostly."

"You're not sympathetic, perhaps."

During the talk Hooper had been to a cupboard and mixed a glass of whisky and soda. He brought it to Beaumaroy and put it on a small table by him. Beaumaroy regarded his squat paunchy figure, red face, small eyes (a squint in one of them), and bulbous nose with a patient and benign toleration.

"Since you can't expect, Sergeant, to prepossess the judge and jury in your favor, the instant you make your appearance in the box—"

"Here, what are you on to, sir?"

"It's the more important for you to have it clearly in your mind that we are laboring in the cause of humanity, freedom, and justice. Exactly like the Allies in the late war, you know, Sergeant. Keep that in your mind, clinch it! He hasn't wanted you to do anything particular to-night, or asked for me?"

"No, sir. He's happy with—with what you call his playthings."

"What are they but playthings?" asked Beaumaroy, tilting his glass to his lips with a smile perhaps a little wry.

"Only I wish as you wouldn't talk about judges and juries," the Sergeant complained.

"I really don't know whether it's a civil or a criminal matter, or both, or neither," Beaumaroy admitted candidly. "But what we do know, Sergeant, is that it provides us with excellent billets and rations. Moreover, a thing that you certainly will not appreciate, it gratifies my taste for the mysterious."

"I hope there's a bit more coming from it than that," said the Sergeant. "That is, if we stick together faithful, sir."

"Oh, we shall! One thing puzzles me about you, Sergeant. I don't think I've mentioned it before. Sometimes you speak almost like an educated man; at others your speech is, well, illiterate."

"Well, sir, it's a sort of mixture of my mother; she was class, the blighter who come after my father, and the Board School—"

"Of course! What they call the educational ladder! That explains it. By the way, I'm thinking of changing our doctor."

"Good job, too. I 'ate that Irechester. Stares at you, that chap does."

"Does he stare at your eyes?'" asked Beaumaroy thoughtfully.

"I don't know that he does at my eyes particularly. Nothing wrong with 'em, is there?" The Sergeant sounded rather truculent.

"Never mind that; but I fancied he stared at Mr. Saffron's. And I've read somewhere, in some book or other, that doctors can tell, or guess, by the eyes. Well, that's only an idea. How does a lady doctor appeal to you, Sergeant?"

"I should be shy," said the Sergeant, grinning.

"Vulgar! vulgar!" Beaumaroy murmured.

"That Dr. Mary Arkroyd?"

"I had thought of her."

"She ought to be fair easy to kid. You 'ave notions sometimes, sir."

Beaumaroy stretched out his legs, debonnair, well-rounded legs, to the seducing blaze of oak logs.

"I haven't really a care in the world," he said.

The Sergeant's reply, or comment, had a disconcerting ring. "And you're sure of 'Eaven? That's what the bloke always says to the 'angman."

"I've no intention of being a murderer, Sergeant." Beaumaroy's eyebrows were raised in gentle protest.

"Once you're in with a job, you never know," his retainer observed darkly.

Beaumaroy laughed. "Oh, go to the devil! and mix me another whisky." Yet a vague uneasiness showed itself on his face; he looked across the room at the evil-shaped man handling the bottles in the cupboard. He made one queer, restless movement of his arms, as though to free himself. Then, in a moment, he sprang from his chair, a glad kindly smile illuminating his face; he bowed in a very courtly fashion, exclaiming, "Ah! here you are, sir? And all well, I hope?"

Mr. Saffron had entered from the door leading to the Tower, carefully closing it after him. Hooper's hand went up to his forehead in the ghost of a military salute, but a sneering smile persisted on his lips. The only notice Mr. Saffron took of him was a jerk of the head towards the passage, an abrupt and ungracious dismissal, which, however, the Sergeant silently accepted and stumped out. The greeting reserved for Beaumaroy was vastly different. Beaumaroy's own cordiality was more than reciprocated. It seemed impossible to doubt that a genuine affection existed between the elder and the younger man, though the latter had not thought fit to mention the fact to Sergeant Hooper.

"A tiring day, my dear Hector, very tiring. I've transacted a lot of business. But never mind that, it will keep. What of your doings?"

Having sat the old man in the big chair by the fire, Beaumaroy sauntered across to the door of the Tower, locked it, and put the key in his pocket. Then he returned to the fire and, standing in front of it, gave a lively and detailed account of his visit to Old Place.

"They appear to be pleasant people, very pleasant. I should like to know them, if it was not desirable for me to live an entirely secluded life." Mr. Saffron's speech was very distinct and clean cut, rather rapid, high in tone but not disagreeable. "You make pure fun of this Miss Wall, as you do of so many things, Hector, but—" he smiled up at Beaumaroy—"inquisitiveness is not our favorite sin just now!"

"She's so indiscriminately inquisitive that it's a thousand to one against her really finding out anything of importance, sir." Beaumaroy sometimes addressed his employer as "Mr. Saffron," but much more commonly he used the respectful "sir." "I think I'm equal to putting Miss Delia Wall off."

"Still she noticed our weekly journeys!"

"Half Inkston goes to town every day, sir, and the rest three times, twice, or once a week. I called her particular attention to the bag, and told her it was for books from Mudie's!"

"Positive statements like that are a mistake." Mr. Saffron spoke with a sudden sharpness, in pointed rebuke. "If I form a right idea of that woman, she's quite capable of going to Mudie's to ask about us."

"By Jove, you're right, sir, and I was wrong. We'd better go and take out a subscription tomorrow; she'll hardly go so far as to ask the date we started it."

"Yes, let that be done. And, remember, no unnecessary talk." His tone grew milder, as though he were mollified by Beaumaroy's ready submission to his reproof. "We have some places to call at to-morrow, have we?"

"They said they'd have some useful addresses ready for us, sir. I'm afraid, though, that we're exhausting the most obvious resources."

"Still, I hope for a few more good consignments. I suppose you remain confident that the Sergeant has no suspicions as regards that particular aspect of the matter?"

"I'm sure of it, up to the present. Of course there might be an accident, but with him and Mrs. Wiles both off the premises at night, it's hardly likely; and I never let the bag out of my sight while it's in the room with them, hardly out of my hand."

"I should like to trust him, but it's hardly fair to put such a strain on his loyalty."

"Much safer not, sir, as long as we're not driven to it. After all though, I believe the fellow is out to redeem his character, his isn't an unblemished record."

"But the work, the physical labor, entailed on you, Hector!"

"Make yourself easy about that, sir. I'm as strong as a horse. The work's good for me. Remember I've had four years' service."

Mr. Saffron smiled pensively. "It would have been funny if we'd met over there! You and I!"

"It would, sir," laughed Beaumaroy. "But that could hardly have happened without some very curious accident."

The old man harked back. "Yes, a few more good consignments, and we can think in earnest of your start." He was warming his hands, thin yellowish hands, at the fire now, and his gaze was directed into it. Looking down on him, Beaumaroy allowed a smile to appear on his lips, a queer smile, which seemed to be compounded of affection, pity, and amusement.

"The difficulties there remain considerable for the present," he remarked.

"They must be overcome." Once again the old man's voice became sharp and even dictatorial.

"They shall be, sir, depend on it." Beaumaroy's air was suddenly confident, almost braggart. Mr. Saffron nodded approvingly. "But, anyhow, I can't very well start till favorable news comes from—"

"Hush!" There was a knock on the door.

"Mrs. Wiles, to lay the table, I suppose."

"Yes! Come in!" He added hastily to Beaumaroy, in an undertone. "Yes, we must wait for that."

Mrs. Wiles entered as he spoke. She was a colorless, negative kind of a woman, fair, fat, flabby, and forty or thereabouts. She had been the ill-used slave of a local carpenter, now deceased by reason of over-drinking; her nature was to be the slave of the nearest male creature, not from affection (her affections were anemic) but rather, as it seemed, from an instinctive desire to shuffle off from herself any responsibility. But, at all events, she was entirely free from Miss Delia Wall's proclivity.

Mr. Saffron rose. "I'll go and wash my hands. We'll dine just as we are, Hector." Beaumaroy opened the door for him; he acknowledged the attention with a little nod, and passed out to the staircase in the narrow passage. Beaumaroy appeared to consider himself absolved from any preparation, for he returned to the big chair and, sinking into it, lit another cigarette. Meanwhile Mrs. Wiles laid the table, and presently Sergeant Hooper appeared with a bottle of golden-tinted wine.

"That, at least, is the real stuff," thought Beaumaroy as he eyed it in pleasurable anticipation. "Where the dear old man got it, I don't know; but in itself it's almost worth all the racket."

And really, in its present stages, so far as its present developments went, the "racket" pleased him. It amused his active brain, besides (as he had said to Mr. Saffron) exercising his active body, though certainly in a rather grotesque and bizarre fashion. The attraction of it went deeper than that. It appealed to some of those tendencies and impulses of his character which had earned such heavy censure from Major-General Punnit and had produced so grave an expression on Captain Alec's handsome face without, however, being, even in that officer's exacting judgment, disgraceful. And, finally, there was the lure of unexplored possibilities, not only material and external, but psychological not only touching what others might do or what might happen to them, but raising also speculation as to what he might do, or what might happen to him at his own hands; for example, how far he would flout authority, defy the usual, and deny the accepted. The love of rebellion, of making foolish the wisdom of the wise, of hampering the orderly and inexorable treatment of people just as, according to the best modern lights, they ought to be treated, this lawless love was strong in Beaumaroy. Not as a principle; it was the stronger for being an instinct, a wayward instinct that might carry him, he scarce knew where.

Mr. Saffron came back, greeted again by Beaumaroy's courtly bow and Hooper's vaguely reminiscent but slovenly military salute. The pair sat down to a homely beefsteak; but the golden tinted wine gurgled into their glasses. But, before they fell to, there was a little incident. A sudden, but fierce, anger seized old Mr. Saffron. In his harshest tones he rapped out at the Sergeant, "My knife! You careless scoundrel, you haven't given me my knife!"

Beaumaroy sprang to his feet with a muttered exclamation: "It's all my fault, sir. I forgot to give it to Hooper. I always lock it up when I go out." He went to a little oak sideboard and unlocked a drawer, then came back to Mr. Saffron's side. "Here it is, and I humbly apologize."

"Very good! very good!" said the old man testily, as he took the implement.

"Ain't anybody going to apologize to me?" asked Hooper, scowling.

"Oh, get out, Sergeant!" said Beaumaroy good-naturedly. "We can't bother about your finer feelings." He glanced anxiously at Mr. Saffron. "All right now, aren't you, sir?" he inquired.

Mr. Saffron drank his glass of wine. "I am perhaps too sensitive to any kind of inattention; but it's not wholly unnatural in my position, Hector."

"We both desire to be attentive and respectful, sir. Don't we, Hooper?"

"Oh my, yes!" grinned the Sergeant, showing his very ugly teeth. "It's only owing that we 'aven't quite been brought up in royal palaces."

Chapter 4

Professional Etiquette

Dr. Irechester was a man of considerable attainments and an active, though not very persevering, intellect. He was widely read both in professional and general literature, but had shrunk from the arduous path of specialization. And he shrank even more from the drudgery of his calling. He had private means, inherited in middle life; his wife had a respectable portion; there was, then, nothing in his circumstances to thwart his tastes and tendencies. He had soon come to see in the late Dr. Evans a means of relief rather than a threat of rivalry; even more easily he slipped into the same way of regarding Mary Arkroyd, helped thereto by a lingering feeling that, after all and in spite of all, when it came to really serious cases, a woman could not, at best, play more than second fiddle. So, as has been seen, he patronized and encouraged Mary; he told himself that, when she had thoroughly proved her capacity—within the limits which he ascribed to it—to take her into partnership would not be a bad arrangement. True, he could pretty well choose his patients now; but as senior partner he would be able to do it completely. It was well-nigh inconceivable that, for example, the Naylors— great friends—should ever leave him; but he would like to be quite secure of the pick of new patients, some of whom might, through ignorance or whim, call in Mary. There was old Saffron, for instance. He was, in Irechester's private opinion, or, perhaps it should be said in his private suspicions, an interesting case; yet, just for that reason, unreliable, and evidently ready to take offense. It was because of cases of that kind that he contemplated offering partnership to Mary; he would both be sure of keeping them and able to devote himself to them.

But his wife laughed at Mary, or at that development of the feminist movement which had produced her and so many other more startling phenomena. The Doctor was fond of his wife, a sprightly, would-be fashionable, still very pretty woman. But her laughter, and the opinion it represented, were to him the merest crackling of thorns under a pot.

The fine afternoon had come, a few days before Christmas, and he sat, side by side with Mr. Naylor, both warmly wrapped in coats and rugs, watching the lawn tennis at Old Place. Doctor Mary and Beaumaroy were playing together, the latter accustoming himself to a finger short in gripping his racquet, against Cynthia and Captain Alec. The Captain could not yet cover the court in his old fashion, but his height and reach made him formidable at the net, and Cynthia was very active. Ten days of Inkston air had made a vast difference to Cynthia. And something else was helping. It required no common loyalty to lost causes and ruined ideals—it is surely not harsh to indicate Captain Cranster by these terms?—to resist Alec Naylor. In fact he had almost taken Cynthia's breath away at their first meeting; she thought that she had never seen anything quite so magnificent, or—all round and from all points of view, so romantic; his stature, handsomeness, limp, renown. Who can be surprised at it? Moreover, he was modest and simple, and no fool within the bounds of his experience.

"She seems a nice little girl, that, and uncommon pretty," Naylor remarked.

"Yes, but he's a queer fish, I fancy," the Doctor answered, also rather absently. Their minds were not running on parallel lines.

"My boy a queer fish?" Naylor expostulated humorously.

Irechester smiled; his lips shut close and tight, his smile was quick but narrow. "You're matchmaking. I was diagnosing," he said.

Naylor apologized. "I've a desperate instinct to fit all these young fellows up with mates as soon as possible. Isn't it only fair?"

"And also extremely expedient. But it's the sort of thing you can leave to them, can't you?"

"As to Beaumaroy—I suppose you meant him, not Alec—I think you must have been talking to old Tom Punnit—or, rather, hearing him talk."

"Punnit's general view is sound enough, I think, as to the man's characteristics; but he doesn't appreciate his cunning."

"Cunning?" Naylor was openly astonished. "He doesn't strike me as a cunning man, not in the least."

"Possibly, possibly, I say—not in his ends, but in his means and expedients. That's my view. I just put it on record, Naylor. I never like talking too much about my cases."

"Beaumaroy's not your patient, is he?"

"His employer, I suppose he's his employer, Saffron is. Well, I thought it advisable to see Saffron alone. I tried to. Saffron was reluctant, this man here openly against it. Next time I shall insist. Because I think, mind you, at present I no more than think, that there's more in Saffron's case than meets the eye."

Naylor glanced at him, smiling. "You fellows are always starting hares," he said.

"Game and set!" cried Captain Alec, and—to his partner—"Thank you very much for carrying a cripple."

But Irechester's attention remained fixed on Beaumaroy, and consequently on Doctor Mary, for the partners did not separate at the end of their game, but, after putting on their coats, began to walk up and down together on the other side of the court, in animated conversation, though Beaumaroy did most of the talking, Mary listening in her usual grave and composed manner. Now and then a word or two reached Irechester's ears, old Naylor seemed to have fallen into a reverie over his cigar, and it must be confessed that he took no pains not to overhear. Once at least he plainly heard "Saffron" from Beaumaroy; he thought that the same lips spoke his own name, and he was sure that Doctor Mary's did. Beaumaroy was speaking rather urgently, and making gestures with his hands; it seemed as though he were appealing to his companion in some difficulty or perplexity. Irechester's mouth was severely compressed and his glance suspicious as he watched.

The scene was ended by Gertie Naylor calling these laggards in to tea, to which meal the rest of the company had already betaken itself.

At the tea table they found General Punnit discoursing on war, and giving "idealists" what idealists usually get. The General believed in war; he pressed the biological argument, did not flinch when Mr. Naylor dubbed him the "British Bernhardi," and invoked the support of "these medical gentleman" (this with a smile at Doctor Mary's expense) for his point of view. War tested, proved, braced, hardened; it was nature's crucible; it was the antidote to softness and sentimentality; it was the vindication of the strong, the elimination of the weak.

"I suppose there's a lot in all that, sir," said Alec Naylor, "but I don't think the effect on one's character is always what you say. I think I've come out of this awful business a good deal softer than I went in." He laughed in an apologetic way. "More, more sentimental, if you like, with more feeling, don't you know, for human life, and suffering, and so on. I've seen a great many men killed, but the sight hasn't made me any more ready to kill men. In fact, quite the reverse." He smiled again. "Really sometimes, for a row of pins, I'd have turned conscientious objector."

Mrs. Naylor looked apprehensively at the General: would he explode? No, he took it quite quietly. "You're a man who can afford to say it, Alec," he remarked, with a nod that was almost approving.

Naylor looked affectionately at his son and turned to Beaumaroy. "And what's the war done to you?" he asked. And this question did draw from the General, if not an explosion, at least a rather contemptuous smile: Beaumaroy had earned no right to express opinions!

But express one he did, and with his habitual air of candor. "I believe it's destroyed every, scruple I ever had!"

"Mr. Beaumaroy!" exclaimed his hostess, scandalized; while the two girls, Cynthia and Gertie, laughed.

"I mean it. Can you see human life treated as dirt, absolutely as cheap as dirt, for three years, and come out thinking it worth anything? Can you fight for your own hand, right or wrong? Oh, yes, right or wrong, in the end, and it's no good blinking it. Can you do that for three years in war, and then hesitate to fight for your own hand, right or wrong, in peace? Who really cares for right or wrong, anyhow?"

A pause ensued—rather an uncomfortable pause. There was a raw sincerity in Beaumaroy's utterance that made it a challenge.

"I honestly think we did care about the rights and wrongs—we in England," said Naylor.

"That was certainly so at the beginning," Irechester agreed.

Beaumaroy took him up smartly. "Aye, at the beginning. But what about when our blood got up? What then? Would we, in our hearts, rather have been right and got a licking, or wrong and given one?"

"A searching question!" mused old Naylor. "What say you, Tom Punnit?"

"It never occurred to me to put the question," the General answered brusquely.

"May I ask why not, sir?" said Beaumaroy respectfully.

"Because I believed in God. I knew that we were right, and I knew that we should win."

"Are we in theology now, or still in biology?" asked Irechester, rather acidly.

"You're getting out of my 'depth anyhow," smiled Mrs. Naylor. "And I'm sure the girls must be bewildered."

"Mamma, I've done biology!"

"And many people think they've done theology!" chuckled Naylor. "Done it completely!"

"I've raised a pretty argument!" said Beaumaroy, smiling. "I'm sorry! I only meant to answer your question about the effect the whole thing has had on myself."

"Even your answer to that was pretty startling, Mr. Beaumaroy," said Doctor Mary, smiling too. "You gave us to understand that it had obliterated for you all distinctions of right and wrong, didn't you?"

"Did I go as far as that?" he laughed. "Then I'm open to the remark that they can't have been very strong at first."

"Now don't destroy the general interest of your thesis," Naylor implored. "It's quite likely that yours is a case as common as Alec's, or even commoner. 'A brutal and licentious soldiery,' isn't that a classic phrase in our histories? All the same, I fancy Mr. Beaumaroy does himself less than justice." He laughed. "We shall be able to judge of that when we know him better."

"At all events, Miss Gertie, look out that I don't fake the score at tennis!" said Beaumaroy.

"A man might be capable of murder, but not capable of that," said Alec.

"A truly British sentiment!" cried his father. "Tom, we have got back to the national ideals."

The discussion ended in laughter, and the talk turned to lighter matters; but, as Mary Arkroyd drove Cynthia home across the heath, her thoughts returned to it. The two men, the two soldiers, seemed to have given an authentic account of what their experience had done to them. Both, as she saw the case, had been moved to pity, horror, and indignation that such things should be done, or should have to be done, in the world. After that point came the divergence. The higher nature had been raised, the lower debased; Alec Naylor's sympathies had been sharpened and sensitized; Beaumaroy's blunted. Where the one had found ideals and incentives, the other found despair—a despair that issued in excuses and denied high standards. And the finer mind belonged to the finer soldier; that she knew, for Gertie had told her General Punnit's story, and, however much she might discount it as the tale of an elderly martinet, yet it stood for something, for something that could never be attributed to Alec Naylor.

And yet, for her mind traveled back to her earlier talk by the tennis court, Beaumaroy had a conscience, had feelings. He was fond of old Mr. Saffron; he felt a responsibility for him, felt it, indeed, keenly. Or was he, under all that seeming openness, a consummate hypocrite? Did he value Mr. Saffron only as a milk cow, the doting giver of a large salary? Was his only desire to humor him, keep him in good health and temper, and use him to his own profit? A puzzling man, but, at all events, cutting a poor figure beside Alec Naylor, about whom there could circle no clouds of doubt. Doctor Mary's learning and gravity did not prevent her from drawing a very heroic and rather romantic figure of Captain Alec—notwithstanding that she sometimes found him rather hard to talk to.

She felt Cynthia's arm steal around her waist, and Cynthia said softly, "I did enjoy my afternoon. Can we go again soon, Mary?"

Mary glanced at her. Cynthia laughed and blushed. "Isn't he splendid?" Cynthia murmured. "But I don't like Mr. Beaumaroy, do you?"

"I say yes to the first question, but I'm not quite ready to answer the second," said Mary with a laugh.

Three days later, on Christmas Eve, one whom Jeanne, who caught sight of him in the hall, described as being all there was possible of ugliness, delivered (with a request for an immediate answer) the following note for Mary Arkroyd:

Dear Dr. Arkroyd:

Mr. Saffron is unwell, and I have insisted that he must see a doctor. So much he has yielded, after a fight! But nothing will induce him to see Dr. Irechester again. On this point I tried to reason with him, but in vain. He is obstinate and resolved. I am afraid that I am putting you in a difficult and disagreeable position, but it seems to me that I have no alternative but to ask you to call on him professionally. I hope that Dr. Irechester will not be hurt by a whim which is, no doubt, itself merely a symptom of disordered nerves, for Dr. Irechester has been most attentive and very successful hitherto in dealing with the dear old gentleman. But my first duty is to Mr. Saffron. If it will ease matters at all, pray hold yourself at liberty to show this note to Dr. Irechester. May I beg you to be kind enough to call at your earliest convenience, though it is, alas, a rough evening to ask you to come out?

Yours very faithfully,

Hector Beaumaroy.

"How very awkward!" exclaimed Mary. She had prided herself on a rigorous abstention from "poaching"; she fancied that men were very ready to accuse women of not "playing the game" and had been resolved to give no color to such an accusation. "Mr. Saffron has sent for me—professionally. He's ill, it seems," she said to Cynthia.

"Why shouldn't he?"

"Because he is a patient of Dr. Irechester, not a patient of mine."

"But people often change their doctors, don't they? He thinks you're cleverer, I suppose, and I expect you are really."

There was no use in expounding professional etiquette to Cynthia. Mary had to decide the point for herself, and quickly; the old man might be seriously ill. Beaumaroy had said at the Naylors' that his attacks were sometimes alarming.

Suddenly she recollected that he had also seemed to hint that they were more alarming than Irechester appeared to appreciate; she had not taken much notice of that hint at the time, but now it recurred to her very distinctly. There was no suggestion of the sort in Beaumaroy's letter. Beaumaroy had written a letter that could be shown to Irechester! Was that dishonesty, or only a pardonable diplomacy?

"I suppose I must go, and explain to Dr. Irechester afterwards." She rang the bell, to recall the maid, and gave her answer. "Say I will be round as soon as possible. Is the messenger walking?"

"He's got a bicycle, Miss."

"All right. I shall be there almost as soon as he is."

She seemed to have no alternative, just as Beaumaroy had none. Yet while she put on her mackintosh, it was very wet and misty, got out her car, and lit her lamps, her face was still fretful and her mind disturbed. For now, as she looked back on it, Beaumaroy's conversation with her at Old Place seemed just a prelude to this summons, and meant to prepare her for it. Perhaps that too was pardonable diplomacy, and no reference to it could be expected in a letter which she was at liberty to show to Dr. Irechester. She wondered, uncomfortably, how Irechester would take it.

Chapter 5

A Familiar Implement

As Mary brought her car to a stand at the gate of the little front garden of Tower Cottage, she saw, through the mist, Beaumaroy's corrugated face; he was standing in the door-way, and the light in the passage revealed it. It seemed to her to wear a triumphant impish look, but this vanished as he advanced to meet her, relieved her of the neat black handbag which she always carried with her on her visits, and suggested gravely that she should at once go upstairs and see her patient.

"He's quieter now," he said. "The mere news that you were coming had a soothing effect. Let me show you the way." He led her upstairs and into a small room on the first floor, nakedly furnished with necessities, but with a cheery fire blazing in the grate.

Old Mr. Saffron lay in bed, propped up by pillows. His silver hair strayed from under a nightcap; he wore a light blue bedroom jacket; its color matched that of his restless eyes; his arms were under the clothes from the elbows down. He was rather flushed, but did not look seriously ill, and greeted Doctor Mary with dignified composure.

"I'll see Dr. Arkroyd alone, Hector." Beaumaroy gave the slightest little jerk of his head, and the old man added quickly, "I am sure of myself, quite sure."

The phrase sounded rather an odd one to Mary, but Beaumaroy accepted the assurance with a nod: "All right, I'll wait downstairs, sir. I hope you'll bring me a good account of him, Doctor." So he left Mary to make her examination; going downstairs, he shook his head once, pursed up his lips, and then smiled doubtfully, as a man may do when he has made up his mind to take a chance.

When Mary rejoined him, she asked for pen and paper, wrote a prescription, and requested that Beaumaroy's man should take it to the chemist's. He went out, to give it to the Sergeant, and, when he came back, found her seated in the big chair by the fire.

"The present little attack is nothing, Mr. Beaumaroy," she said. "Stomachic—with a little fever; if he takes what I've prescribed, he ought to be all right in the morning. But I suppose you know that there is valvular disease—quite definite? Didn't Dr. Irechester tell you?"

"Yes; but he said there was no particular—no immediate danger."

"If he's kept quiet and free from worry. Didn't he advise that?"

"Yes," Beaumaroy admitted, "he did. That's the only thing you find wrong with him, Doctor?"

Beaumaroy was standing on the far side of the table, his finger-tips resting lightly on it. He looked across at Mary with eyes candidly inquiring.

"I've found nothing else so far. I suppose he's got nothing to worry him?"

"Not really, I think. He fusses a bit about his affairs." He smiled. "We go to London every week to fuss about his affairs; he's always changing his investments, taking his money out of one thing and putting it in another, you know. Old people get like that sometimes, don't they? I'm a novice at that kind of thing, never having had any money to play with; but I'm bound to say that he seems to know very well what he's about."

"Do you know anything of his history or his people? Has he any relations?"

"I know very little. I don't think he has any, any real relations, so to speak. There are, I believe, some cousins, distant cousins, whom he hates. In fact, a lonely old bachelor, Dr. Arkroyd."

Mary gave a little laugh and became less professional. "He's rather an old dear! He uses funny stately phrases. He said I might speak quite openly to you, as you were closely attached to his person!"

"Sounds rather like a newspaper, doesn't it? He does talk like that sometimes." Beaumaroy moved round the table, came close to the fire, and stood there, smiling down at Mary.

"He's very fond of you, I think," she went on.

"He reposes entire confidence in me," said Beaumaroy, with a touch of assumed pompousness.

"Those were his very words!" cried Mary, laughing again. "And he said it just in that way! How clever of you to guess!"

"Not so very. He says it to me six times a week."

Mary had risen, about to take her leave, but to her surprise Beaumaroy went on quickly, with one of his confidential smiles, "And now I'm going to show you that I have the utmost confidence in you. Please sit down again, Dr. Arkroyd. The matter concerns your patient just as much as myself, or I wouldn't trouble you with it, at any rate I shouldn't venture to so early in our acquaintance. I want you to consider yourself as Mr. Saffron's medical adviser, and, also, to try to imagine yourself my friend."

"I've every inclination to be your friend, but I hardly know you, Mr. Beaumaroy."

"And feel a few doubts about me? From what you've heard from myself, and perhaps from others?"

The wind swished outside; save for that, the little room seemed very still. The professional character of the interview did not save it, for Mary Arkroyd, from a sudden and rather unwelcome sense of intimacy, of an intimacy thrust upon her, though not so much by her companion as by circumstances. She answered rather stiffly, "Perhaps I have some doubts."

"You detect, very acutely, that I have a great influence over Mr. Saffron. You ask, very properly, whether he has relations. I think you threw out a feeler about his money affairs, whether he had anything to worry about was your phrase, wasn't it? Am I misinterpreting what was in your mind?"

As he spoke, he offered her a cigarette from a box on the mantelpiece. She took one and lit it at the top of the lamp-chimney; then she sat down again in the big chair; she had not accepted his earlier invitation to resume her seat.

"It was proper for me to put those questions, Mr. Beaumaroy. Mr. Saffron is not a sound man, and he's old. In normal conditions his relations should at least be warned of the position."

46

"Exactly," Beaumaroy assented with an appearance of eagerness. "But he hates them. Any suggestion that they have any sort of claim on him raises strong resentment in him. I've known old men, old moneyed men, like that before, and no doubt you have. Well now, you'll begin to see the difficulty of my position. I'll put the case to you quite bluntly. Suppose Mr. Saffron, having this liking for me, this confidence in me, living here with me alone, except for servants; being, as one might say, exposed to my influence; suppose he took it into his head to make a will in my favor, to leave me all his money. It's quite a considerable sum, so far as our Wednesday doings enable me to judge. Suppose that happened, how should I stand in your opinion, Dr. Arkroyd? But wait a moment still. Suppose that my career has not been very, well, resplendent; that my army record is only so-so; that I've devoted myself to him with remarkable assiduity, as in fact I have; that I might be called, quite plausibly, an adventurer. Well, propounding that will, how should I stand before the world and, if necessary (he shrugged his shoulders), the Court?"

Mary sat silent for a moment or two. Beaumaroy knelt down by the fire, rearranged the logs of wood which were smouldering there, and put on a couple more. From that position, looking into the grate, he added, "And the change of doctors? It was he, of course, who insisted on it, but I can see a clever lawyer using that against me too. Can't you, Dr. Arkroyd?"

"I'm sure I wish you hadn't had to make the change!" exclaimed Mary.

"So do I; though, mind you, I'm not pretending that Irechester is a favorite of mine, any more than he is of my old friend's. Still, there it is. I've no right, perhaps, to press my question, but your opinion would be of real value to me."

"I see no reason to think that he's not quite competent to make a will," said Doctor Mary. "And no real reason why he shouldn't prefer you to distant relations whom he dislikes."

"Ah, no real reason; that's what you say! You mean that people would impute—"

Mary Arkroyd had her limitations—of experience, of knowledge, of intuition. But she did not lack courage.

"I have given you my professional opinion. It is that, so far as I see, Mr. Saffron is of perfectly sound understanding, and capable of making a valid will. You did me the honor—"

"No, no!" he interrupted in a low but rather strangely vehement protest. "I begged the favor—"

"As you like! The favor then, of asking me to give you my opinion as your friend, as well as my view as Mr. Saffron's doctor."

Beaumaroy did not rise from his knees, but turned his face towards her; the logs had blazed up, and his eyes looked curiously bright in the glare, themselves, as it were, afire.

"In my opinion a man of sensitive honor would prefer that that will should not be made, Mr. Beaumaroy," said Mary steadily.

Beaumaroy appeared to consider. "I'm a bit posed by that point of view, Dr. Arkroyd," he said at last, "Either the old man's sane—*compos mentis,* don't you call it?—or he isn't. If he is—"

"I know. But I feel that way about it."

"You'd have to give evidence for me!" He raised his brows and smiled at her.

"There can be undue influence without actual want of mental competence, I think."

"I don't know whether my influence is undue. I believe I'm the only creature alive who cares twopence for the poor old gentleman."

"I know! I know! Mr. Beaumaroy, your position is very difficult. I see that. It really is. But, would you take the money for yourself? Aren't you—well, rather in the position of a trustee?"

"Who for? The hated cousins? What's the reason in that?"

"They may be very good people really. Old men take fancies, as you said yourself. And they may have built on—"

"Stepping into a dead man's shoes? I dare say. Why mayn't I build on it too? Why not my hand against the other fellow's?"

"That's what you learnt from the war! You said so—at Old Place. Captain Naylor said something different."

"Suppose Alec Naylor and I, a hero and a damaged article," he smiled at Mary, and she smiled back with a sudden enjoyment of the humorous yet bitter tang in his voice, "loved the same woman, and I had a chance of her. Am I to give it up?"

"Really we're getting a long way from medicine, Mr. Beaumaroy!"

"Oh, you're a general practitioner! Wise on all subjects under heaven! Conceive yourself hesitating between him and me—"

Mary laughed frankly. "How absurd you are! If you must go on talking, talk seriously."

"But why am I absurd?"

"Because, if I were a marrying woman, which I'm not, I shouldn't hesitate between you and Captain Naylor, not for a minute."

"You'd jump at me?"

Laughing again, his eyes had now a schoolboy merriment in them, Mary rose from the big chair. "At him, if I'm not being impolite, Mr. Beaumaroy."

They stood face to face. For the first time for several years—Mary's girlhood had not been altogether empty of sentimental episodes—she blushed under a man's glance, because it was a man's. At this event, of which she was acutely conscious and at which she was intensely irritated, she drew herself up, with an attempt to return to her strictly professional manner.

"I don't find you the least impolite, Dr. Arkroyd," said Beaumaroy.

It was impudent, yet gay, dexterous, and elusive enough to avoid reproof. With no more than a little shake of her head and a light yet embarrassed laugh, Mary moved toward the door, her way lying between the table and an old oak sideboard, which stood against the wall. Some plates, knives, and other articles of the table lay strewn, none too tidily, about it. Beaumaroy followed her, smiling complacently, his hands in his pockets.

Suddenly Mary came to a stop and pointed with her finger at the sideboard, turning her face towards her companion. At the same instant Beaumaroy's right hand shot out from his pocket towards the sideboard, as though to snatch up something from it. Then he drew the hand as swiftly back again; but his eyes watched Mary's with an alert and suspicious gaze. That was for a second only;

then his face resumed its amused and nonchalant expression. But the movement of the hand and the look of the eyes had not escaped Mary's attention; her voice betrayed some surprise as she said:

"It's only that I just happened to notice that combination knife-and-fork lying there, and I wondered who—"

The article in question lay among some half-dozen ordinary knives and forks. It was of a kind quite familiar to Doctor Mary from her hospital experience, a fork on one side, a knife-blade on the other; an implement made for people who could command the use of only one hand.

"Surely you've noticed my hand?" He drew his right hand again from the pocket to which he had so quickly returned it. "I used to use that in hospital, when I was bandaged up. But that's a long while ago now, and I can't think why Hooper's left it lying there."

The account was plausible, and entirely the same might now be said of his face and manner. But Mary had seen the dart of his hand and the sudden alertness in his eyes. Her own rested on him for a moment with inquiry, for the first time with a hint of distrust. "I see!" she murmured vaguely, and, turning away from him, pursued her way to the door. Beaumaroy followed her with a queer smile on his lips; he shrugged his shoulders once, very slightly.

A constraint had fallen on Mary. She allowed herself to be escorted to the car and helped into it in silence. Beaumaroy made no effort to force the talk, possibly by reason of the presence of Sergeant Hooper, who had arrived back from the chemist's with the medicine for Mr. Saffron just as Mary and Beaumaroy came out of the hall door. He stood by his bicycle, drawing just a little aside to let them pass, but not far enough to prevent the light from the passage showing up his ill-favored countenance.

"Well, good-bye, Dr. Arkroyd. I'll see how he is to-morrow, and ask you to be kind enough to call again, if it seems advisable. And a thousand thanks."

"Good-night, Mr. Beaumaroy."

She started the car. Beaumaroy walked back to the hall door. Mary glanced behind her once, and saw him standing by it, again framed by the light behind him, as she had seen him on her arrival. But, this time, within the four corners of the same frame was included the forbidding visage of Sergeant Hooper.

Beaumaroy returned to the fire in the parlor; Hooper, leaving his bicycle in the passage, followed him into the room and put the medicine bottle on the table. Smiling at him, Beaumaroy pointed at the combination knife-and-fork.

"Is it your fault or mine that that damned thing's lying there?" he asked.

"Yours," answered the Sergeant without hesitation and with his habitual surliness. "I cleaned it and put it out for you to lock away, as usual. Suppose you went and forgot it, sir!"

Beaumaroy shook his head in self-condemnation and a humorous dismay. "That's it! I went and forgot it, Sergeant. And I think, I rather think, that Doctor Mary smells a rat, though she is, at present, far from guessing the color of the animal!"

The words sounded scornful; they were spoken for the Sergeant as well as for himself. He was looking amused and kindly, even rather tenderly amused; as though liking and pity were the emotions which most actively survived his first private conversation with Doctor Mary, in spite of that mishap of the combination knife-and-fork.

Chapter 6

Odd Story of Captain Duggle

Christmas Day of 1918 was a merry feast, and nowhere merrier than at Old Place. There was a house-party and, for dinner on the day itself, a local contingent as well: Miss Wall, the Irechesters, Mr. Penrose, and Doctor Mary. Mr. Beaumaroy also had been invited by Mrs. Naylor; she considered him an interesting man and felt pity for the obvious *ennui* of his situation; but he had not felt able to leave his old friend. Doctor Mary's Paying Guest was of the house-party, not merely a dinner guest. She was asked over to spend three days and went, accompanied by Jeanne, who by this time was crying much less; crying was no longer the cue; her mistress, and not merely stern Doctor Mary, had plainly shown her that. Gertie Naylor had invited Cynthia to help her in entertaining the sub-alterns, though Gertie was really quite equal to that task herself; there were only three of them, and if a pretty girl is not equal to three subalterns, well, what are we coming to in England? And, as it turned out, Miss Gertie had to deal with them all, sometimes collectively, sometimes one by one, practically unassisted. Cynthia was otherwise en-gaged. Gertie complained neither of the cause nor of its consequence.

The drink, or drugs, hypothesis was exploded, and Miss Wall's speculations set at rest, with a quite comforting solatium of romantic and unhappy interest, "a nice tit-bit for the old cat," as Mr. Naylor unkindly put it. Cynthia had told her story; she wanted a richer sympathy than Doctor Mary's common-sense afforded; out of this need the revelation came to Gertie in innocent confidence, and, with the narrator's tacit approval, ran through the family and its intimate friends. If Cynthia had been as calculating as she was guileless, she could not have done better for herself. Mrs. Naylor's motherliness, old Naylor's courtliness, Gertie's breathless concern and avid appetite for the fullest detail, everybody's desire to console and cheer, all these were at her service, all enlisted in the effort to make her forget, and live and laugh again. Her heart responded; she found herself becoming happy at a rate which made her positively ashamed. No wonder tactful Jeanne discovered that the cue was changed!

Fastidious old Naylor regarded his wife with the affection of habit and with a little disdain for the ordinariness of her virtues—not to say of the mind which they adorned. His daughter was to him a precious toy, on which he tried jokes, played tricks, and lavished gifts, for the joy of seeing the prettiness of her reactions to his treatment. It never occurred to him to think that his toy might be broken; fond as he was, his feeling for her lacked the apprehensiveness of the deepest love. But he idolized his son, and in this case neither without fear nor without understanding. For four years now he had feared for him bitterly: for his body, for his life. At every waking hour his inner cry had been even as David's, "Would God I had died for thee, my son, my son!" For at every moment of those four years it might be that his son was even then dead. That terror, endured under a cool and almost off-hand demeanor, was past; but he feared for his son still. Of all who went to the war as Crusaders, none had the temperament more ardently than Alec. As he went, so, obviously, he had come back, not dis-illusioned, nay, with all his illusions, or delusions, about this wicked world and its possibilities, about the people who dwell in it and their lamentable limitations, stronger in his mind than ever. How could he get through life with-out being too sorely hurt and wounded, without being cut to the very quick by his inevitable discoveries? Old Naylor did not see how it was to be done, or even hoped for; but the right kind of wife was unquestionably the best chance.

He had cast a speculative eye on Cynthia Walford, Irechester had caught him at it, but, as he observed her more, she did not altogether satisfy him. Alec needed someone more stable, stronger, someone in a sense protec-tive; somebody more like Mary Arkroyd; that idea passed through his thoughts; if only Mary would take the trouble to dress herself, remember that she was, or might be made, an attractive young woman; and, yes, throw her mortar and pestle out of the window without, however, discarding with them the sturdy, sane, balanced qualities of mind which enabled her to handle them with such ad-mirable competence. But he soon had to put this idea from him. His son's own impulse was to give, not to seek, pro-tection and support.

Of Cynthia's woeful experience Alec had spoken to his father once only: "It makes me mad to think the fellow who did that wore a British uniform!"

How unreasonable! Since by all the laws of average, when millions of men are wearing a uniform, there must be some rogues in it. But it was Alec's way to hold himself responsible for the whole of His Majesty's Forces. Their honor was his; for their misdeeds he must in his own person make reparation. "That fellow Beaumaroy may have lost his conscience, but my boy seems to have acquired five million," the old man grumbled to himself—a grumble full of pride.

The father might analyze; with Alec it was all impulse, the impulse to soothe, to obliterate, to atone. The girl had been sorely hurt; with the acuteness of sympathy he divined that she felt herself in a way soiled and stained by contact with unworthiness and by a too easy acceptance of it. All that must be swept out of her heart, out of her memory, if it could be.

Doctor Mary saw what was happening, and with a little pang to which she would not have liked to own. She had set love affairs, and all the notions connected therewith, behind her; but she had idealized Alec Naylor a little; and she thought Cynthia, in homely phrase, "hardly good enough." Was it not rather perverse that the very fact of having been a little goose should help her to win so rare a swan?

"You're taking my patient out of my hands, Captain Alec!" she said to him jokingly. "And you're devoting great attention to the case."

He flushed. "She seems to like to talk to me," he answered simply. "She seems to me to have rather a remarkable mind, Doctor Mary." (She was "Doctor Mary" to all the Old Place party now, in affection, with a touch of chaff.)

O sancta simplicitas! Mary longed to say; that Cynthia was a very ordinary child. Like to talk to him, indeed! Of course she did; and to use her girl's weapons on him; and to wonder, in an almost awestruck delight, at their effect on this dazzling hero. Well, the guilelessness of heroes!

So mused Mary, on the unprofessional side of her mind, as she watched, that Christmastide, Captain Alec's delicate, sensitively indirect, and delayed approach toward the ripe fruit that hung so ready to his hand. "Part of his chivalry to assume she can't think of him yet!" Mary was half-impatient, half-reluctantly admiring; not an uncommon mixture of feeling for the extreme forms of virtue to produce. In the net result, however, her marked image of Alec lost something of its heroic proportions.

But professionally (the distinction must not be pushed too far, she was not built in watertight compartments) Tower Cottage remained obstinately in the center of her thoughts; and, connected with it, there arose a puzzle over Dr. Irechester's demeanor. She had taken advantage of Beaumaroy's permission, though rather doubtful whether she was doing right, for she was still inexperienced in niceties of etiquette, and sent on the letter, with a frank note explaining her own feelings and the reason which had caused her to pay her visit to Mr. Saffron. But though Irechester was quite friendly when they met at Old Place before dinner, and talked freely to her during a rather prolonged period of waiting (Captain Alec and Cynthia, Gertie and two subalterns were very late, having apparently forgotten dinner in more refined delights), he made no reference to the letters, nor to Tower Cottage or its inmates. Mary herself was too shy to break the ice, but wondered at his silence, and the more because the matter evidently had not gone out of his mind. For after dinner, when the port had gone round once and the proper healths been honored, he said across the table to Mr. Penrose:

"We were talking the other day of the Tower, on the heath, you know, by old Saffron's cottage, and none of us knew its history. You know all about Inkston from time out o' mind. Have you got any story about it?"

Mr. Penrose practiced as a solicitor in London, but lived in a little old house near the Irechesters' in the village street, and devoted his leisure to the antiquities and topography of the neighborhood; his lore was plentiful and curious, if not important. He was a small, neat old fellow, with white whiskers of the antique cut, a thin voice, and a dry cackling laugh.

"There was a story about it, and one quite fit for Christmas evening, if you're in the mood to hear it."

The thin voice was penetrating. At the promise of a story silence fell on the company, and Mr. Penrose told his tale, vouching as his authority an erstwhile "oldest inhabitant," now gathered to his fathers; for the tale dated back some eighty years, to the date of the ancient's early manhood.

A seafaring man had suddenly appeared, out of space, as it were, at Inkston, and taken the cottage. He carried with him a strong smell of rum and tobacco, and gave it to be understood that his name was Captain Duggle. He was no beauty, and his behavior was worse than his looks. To that quiet village, in those quiet strait-laced times, he was a horror and a portent. He not only drank prodigiously—that, being in character and also a source of local profit, might have passed with mild censure—but he swore and blasphemed horribly, spurning the parson, mocking at Revelation, even at the Deity Himself. The Devil was his friend, he said. A most terrible fellow, this Captain Duggle. Inkston's hair stood on end, and no wonder!

"No doubt they shivered with delight over it all," commented Mr. Naylor.

Captain Duggle lived all by himself—well, what God-fearing Christian, male or female, would be found to live with him—came and went mysteriously and capriciously, always full of money, and at least equally full of drink! What he did with himself nobody knew, but evil legends gathered about him. Terrified wayfarers, passing the cottage by night, took oath that they had heard more than one voice!

"This is proper Christmas!" a subaltern interjected into Gertie's ear.

Mr. Penrose, with an air of gratification, continued his narrative.

"The story goes on to tell," he said, "of a final interview with the village clergyman, in which that reverend man, as in duty bound, solemnly told Captain Duggle that however much he might curse, and blaspheme, and drink, and, er, do all the other things that the Captain did (obviously here Mr. Penrose felt hampered by the presence of ladies), yet Death, Judgment, and Churchyard wait for him at last. Whereupon the Captain, emitting an inconceivably terrific imprecation, which no one ever dared to repeat and which consequently is lost to tradition, declared that the first he'd never feared, the second was parson's gabble, and as to the third, never should his dead toes be nearer any church than for the last forty years his living feet had been! If so be as he wasn't drowned at sea, he'd make a grave for himself!"

Mr. Penrose paused, sipped port wine, and resumed.

"And so, no doubt, he did, building the Tower for that purpose. By bribes and threats he got two men to work for him. One was the uncle of my informant. But though he built that Tower, and inside it dug his grave, he never lay there, being, as things turned out, carried off by the Devil. Oh, yes, there was no doubt! He went home one night, a Saturday, very drunk, as usual. On the Sunday night a belated wayfarer, possibly also drunk, heard wild shrieks and saw a strange red glow through the window of the Tower, now, by the way, boarded up. And no doubt he'd have smelt brimstone if the wind hadn't set the wrong way! Anyhow Captain Duggle was never seen again by mortal eyes, at Inkston, at all events. After a time the landlord of the cottage screwed up his courage to resume possession; the Captain had only a lease of it, though he built the Tower at his own charges, and, I believe, without any permission, the landlord being much too frightened to interfere with him. He found everything in a sad mess in the house, while in the Tower itself every blessed stick had been burnt up. So the story looks pretty plausible."

"And the grave?" This question came eagerly from at least three of the company.

"In front of the fireplace there was a big oblong hole—six feet by three, by four—planks at the bottom, the sides roughly lined with brick. Captain Duggle's grave; but he wasn't in it!"

"But what really became of him, Mr. Penrose?" cried Cynthia.

"The Rising Generation is very skeptical," said old Naylor. "You, of course, Penrose, believe the story?"

"I do," said Mr. Penrose composedly. "I believe that a devil carried him off, and that its name was *delirium tremens*. We can guess, can't we, Irechester, why he smashed or burnt everything, and fled in mad terror into the darkness? Where to? Was he drowned at sea, or did he take his life, or did he rot to death in some filthy hole? Nobody knows. But the grave he dug is there in the Tower, unless it's been filled up since old Saffron has lived there."

"Why in the world wasn't it filled up before?" asked Alec Naylor with a laugh. "People lived in the cottage, didn't they?"

"I've visited the cottage often," Irechester interposed, "when various people had it, but I never saw any signs of the Tower being used."

"It never was, I'm sure; and as for the grave, well, Alec, in country parts, to this day, you'd be thought a bold man if you filled up a grave that your neighbor had dug for himself, and such a neighbor as Captain Duggle! He might take it into his head some night to visit it, and if he found it filled up there'd be trouble, nasty trouble!" His laugh cackled out rather uncomfortably. Gertie shivered, and one of the subalterns gulped down his port.

"Old Saffron's a man of education, I believe. No doubt he pays no heed to such nonsense, and has had the thing covered up," said Naylor.

"As to that I don't know. Perhaps you do, Irechester? He's your patient, isn't he?"

Dr. Irechester sat four places from Mary. Before he replied to the question he cast a glance at her, smiling rather mockingly. "I've attended him on one or two occasions, but I've never seen the inside of the Tower. So I don't know either."

"Oh, but I'm curious! I shall ask Mr. Beaumaroy," cried Cynthia.

The ironical character of Irechester's smile grew more pronounced, and his voice was at its driest: "Certainly you can ask Beaumaroy, Miss Walford. As far as asking goes, there's no difficulty."

A pause followed this pointed remark, on which nobody seemed disposed to comment. Mrs. Naylor ended the session by rising from her chair.

But Mary Arkroyd was disquieted, worried as to how she stood with Irechester, vaguely but insistently worried over the whole Tower Cottage business. Well, the first point she could soon settle, or try to settle, anyhow.

With the directness which marked her action when once her mind was made up, she waylaid Irechester as he came into the drawing-room; her resolute approach sufficed to detach Naylor from him; he found himself for the moment isolated from everybody except Mary.

"You got my letter, Dr. Irechester? I—I rather expected an answer."

"Your conduct was so obviously and punctiliously correct," he replied suavely, "that I thought my answer could wait till I met you here to-day, as I knew that I was to have the pleasure of doing." He looked her full in the eyes. "You were placed, my dear colleague, in a position in which you had no alternative."

"I thought so, Dr. Irechester, but—"

"Oh yes, clearly! I'm far from making any complaint." He gave her a courteous little bow, but it was one which plainly closed the subject. Indeed he passed by her and joined a group that had gathered on the hearthrug, leaving her alone.

So she stood for a minute, oppressed by a growing uneasiness. Irechester said nothing, but surely meant something of import? He mocked her, but not idly or out of wantonness. He seemed almost to warn her. What could there be to warn her about? He had laid an odd empha-sis on the word "placed"; he had repeated it. Who had "placed" her there? Mr. Saffron? Or—

Alec Naylor broke in on her uneasy meditation. "It's a clinking night, Doctor Mary," he observed. "Do you mind if I walk Miss Walford home, instead of her going with you in your car, you know? It's only a couple of miles and—"

"Do you think your leg can stand it?"

He laughed. "I'll cut the thing off, if it dares to make any objection!"

Chapter 7

A Gentlemanly Stranger

On this same Christmas Day Sergeant Hooper was feeling morose and discontented; not because he was alone in the world (a situation comprising many advantages), nor on the score of his wages, which were extremely liberal; nor on account of the "old blighter's"—that is, Mr. Saffron's—occasional outbursts of temper, these being in the nature of the case and within the terms of the contract; nor, finally, by reason of Beaumaroy's airy insolence, since from his youth up the Sergeant was hardened to unfavorable comments on his personal appearance, trifling vulgarities which a man of sense could afford to ignore.

No; the winter of his discontent—a bitter winter—was due to the conviction, which had been growing in his mind for some time, that he was only in half the secret, and that not the more profitable half. He knew that the old blighter had to be humored in certain small ways, as, for example, in regard to the combination knife-and-fork—and the reason for it. But, first, he did not know what happened inside the Tower; he had never seen the inside of it; the door was always locked; he was never invited to accompany his masters when they repaired thither by day, and he was not on the premises by night. And, secondly, he did not understand the Wednesday journeys to London, and he had never seen the inside of Beaumaroy's brown bag—that, like the Tower door, was always locked. He had handled it once, just before the pair set out for London one Wednesday. Beaumaroy, a careless man sometimes, in spite of the cunning which Dr. Irechester attributed to him, had left it on the parlor table while he helped Mr. Saffron on with his coat in the passage, and the Sergeant had swiftly and surreptitiously lifted it up. It was very light, obviously empty, or, at all events, holding only featherweight contents. He had never got near it when it came back from town; then it always went straight into the Tower and had the key turned on it forthwith.

But the Sergeant, although slow-witted as well as ugly, had had his experiences; he had carried weights both in the army and in other institutions which are officially described as His Majesty's, and had seen other men carry them too. From the set of Beaumaroy's figure as he arrived home on at least two occasions with the brown bag, and from the way in which he handled it, the Sergeant confidently drew the conclusion that it was of a considerable, almost a grievous, weight. What was the heavy thing in it? What became of that thing after it was taken into the Tower? To whose use or profit did it, or was it, to inure? Certainly it was plain, even to the meanest capacity, that the contents of the bag had a value in the eyes of the two men who went to London for them and who shepherded them from London to the custody of the Tower.

These thoughts filled and racked his brain as he sat drinking rum and water in the bar of the *Green Man* on Christmas evening; a solitary man, mixing little with the people of the village, he sat apart at a small table in the corner, musing within himself, yet idly watching the company—villagers, a few friends from London and elsewhere, some soldiers and their ladies. Besides these, a tall slim man stood leaning against the bar, at the far end of it, talking to Bill Smithers, the landlord, and sipping whisky-and-soda between pulls at his cigar. He wore a neat dark overcoat, brown shoes, and a bowler hat rather on one side; his appearance was, in fact, genteel, though his air was a trifle raffish. In age he seemed about forty. The Sergeant had never seen him before, and therefore favored him with a glance of special attention.

Oddly enough, the gentlemanly stranger seemed to reciprocate the Sergeant's interest; he gave him quite a long glance. Then he finished his whisky-and-soda, spoke a word to Bill Smithers, and lounged across the room to where the Sergeant sat.

"It's poor work drinking alone on Christmas night," he observed. "May I join you? I've ordered a little something, and, well, we needn't bother about offering a gentleman a glass tonight."

The Sergeant eyed him with apparent disfavor—as, indeed, he did everybody who approached him—but a nod of his head accorded the desired permission. Smithers came across with a bottle of brandy and glasses. "Good stuff!" said the stranger, as he sat down, filled the glasses, and drank his off. "The best thing to top up with, believe me!"

The Sergeant, in turn, drained his glass, maintaining, however, his aloofness of demeanor. "What's up?" he growled.

"What's in the brown bag?" asked the stranger lightly and urbanely.

The Sergeant did not start; he was too old a hand for that; but his small gimlet eyes searched his new acquaintance's face very keenly. "You know a lot!"

"More than you do in some directions, less in others, perhaps. Shall I begin? Because we've got to confide in one another, Sergeant. A little story of what two gentlemen do in London on Wednesdays, and of what they carry home in a brown leather bag? Would that interest you? Oh, that stuff in the brown leather bag! Hard to come by now, isn't it? But they know where there's still some, and so do I, to remark it incidentally. There were actually some people, Sergeant Hooper, who distrusted the righteousness of the British Cause, which is to say (the stranger smiled cynically) the certainty of our licking the Germans, and they hoarded it, the villains!"

Sergeant Hooper stretched out his hand towards the bottle. "Allow me!" said the stranger politely. "I observe that your hand trembles a little."

It did. The Sergeant was excited. The stranger seemed to be touching on a subject which always excited the Sergeant—to the point of hands trembling, twitching, and itching.

"Have to pay for it, too! Thirty bob in curl-twisters for every ruddy disc; that's the figure now, or thereabouts. What do they want to do it for? What's your governor's game? Who, in short, is going to get off with it?"

"What is it they does, the old blighter and Boomery (thus he pronounced the name Beaumaroy), in London?"

"First to the stockbroker's, then to a bank or two, I've known it three even; then a taxi down East, and a call at certain addresses. The bag's with 'em, Sergeant, and at each call it gets heavier. I've seen it swell, so to speak."

"Who in hell are you?" the Sergeant grunted huskily.

"Names later—after the usual guarantees of good faith."

The whole conversation, carried on in low tones, had passed under cover of noisy mirth, snatches of song, banter, and gigglings; nobody paid heed to the two men talking in a corner. Yet the stranger lowered his voice to a whisper, as he added:

"From me to you fifty quid on account; from you to me just a sight of the place where they put it."

Sergeant Hooper drank, smoked, and pondered. The stranger showed the edge of a roll of notes, protruding it from his breast-pocket. The Sergeant nodded, he understood that part. But there was much that he did not understand. "It fair beats me what the blazes they're doing it *for*," he broke out.

"Whose money would it be?"

"The old blighter's, o' course. Boomery's stony, except for his screw." He looked hard at the gentlemanly stranger, and a slow smile came on his lips, "That's your idea, is it, mister?"

"Gentleman's old, looks frail, might go off suddenly. What then? Friends turn up, always do when you're dead, you know. Well, what of it? Less money in the funds than was reckoned; dear old gentleman doesn't cut up as well as they hoped! And meanwhile our friend B—! Does it dawn on you at all, from our friend B—'s point of view, Sergeant? I may be wrong, but that's my provisional conjecture. The question remains how he's got the old gent into the game, doesn't it?"

Precisely the point to which the Sergeant's mind also had turned! The knowledge which he possessed—that half of the secret—and which his companion did not, might be very material to a solution of the problem; the Sergeant did not mean to share it prematurely, without necessity, or for nothing. But surely it had a bearing on the case? Dull-witted as he was, the Sergeant seemed to catch a glimmer of light, and mentally groped towards it.

"Well, we can't sit here all night," said the stranger in good-humored impatience. "I've a train to catch."

"There's no train up from here to-night."

"There is from Sprotsfield. I shall walk over."

The Sergeant smiled. "Oh, if you're walking to Sprotsfield, I'll put you on your way. If anybody was to see us, Boomery, for instance, he couldn't complain of my seeing an old pal on his way on Christmas night. No 'arm in that; no look of prowling, or spying, or such like! And you are an old pal, ain't you?"

"Certainly; your old pal—let me see—your old pal Percy Bennett."

"As it might he, or as it might not. What about the—" He pointed to Percy Bennett's breast-pocket.

"I'll give it you outside. You don't want me to be seen handing it over in here, do you?"

The Sergeant had one more question to ask. "About 'ow much d'ye reckon there might be by now?"

"How often have they been to London? Because they don't come to see my friends every time, I fancy."

"Must 'ave been six or seven times by now. The game began soon after Boomery and I came 'ere."

"Then, quite roughly, quite a shot, from what I know of the deals we—my friends, I mean—did with them, and reasoning from that, there might be a matter of seven or eight thousand pounds."

The Sergeant whistled softly, rose, and led the way to the door. The gentlemanly stranger paused at the bar to pay for the brandy, and after bidding the landlord a civil good-evening, with the compliments of the season, followed the Sergeant into the village street.

Fifteen minutes' brisk walk brought them to Hinton Avenue. At the end of it they passed Doctor Mary's house; the drawing-room curtains were not drawn; on the blind they saw reflected the shadows of a man and a girl, standing side by side. "Mistletoe, eh?" remarked the stranger. The Sergeant spat on the road; they resumed their way, pursuing the road across the heath.

It was fine, but overclouded and decidedly dark. Every now and then Bennett, to call the stranger by what was almost confessedly a *nom-de-guerre,* flashed a powerful electric torch on the roadway. "Don't want to walk into a gorse-bush," he explained with a laugh.

"Put it away, you darned fool! We're nearly there."

The stranger obeyed. In another seven or eight minutes there loomed up, on the left hand, the dim outline of Mr. Saffron's abode—the square cottage with the odd round tower annexed.

"There you are!" The Sergeant's voice instinctively kept to a whisper. "That's what you want to see."

"But I can't see it—not so as to get any clear idea."

No lights showed from the cottage, nor, of course, from the Tower; its only window had been, as Mr. Penrose said, boarded up. The wind—there was generally a wind on the heath—stirred the fir-trees and the bushes into a soft movement and a faint murmur of sound. A very acute and alert ear might perhaps have caught another sound— footfalls on the road, a good long way behind them. The two spies, or scouts, did not hear them; their attention was elsewhere.

"Probably they're both in bed; it's quite safe to make our examination," said the stranger.

"Yes, I s'pose it is. But look to be ready to douse your glim. Boomery's a nailer at turning up unexpected." The Sergeant seemed rather nervous.

Mr. Bennett was not. He took out his torch, and guided by its light (which, however, he took care not to throw towards the cottage windows) he advanced to the garden gate, the Sergeant following, and took a survey of the premises. It was remarkable that, as the light of the torch beamed out, the faint sound of footfalls on the road behind died away.

"Keep an eye on the windows, and touch my elbow if any light shows. Don't speak." The stranger was at business—his business—now, and his voice became correspondingly businesslike. "We won't risk going inside the gate. I can see from here." Indeed he very well could; Tower Cottage stood back no more than twelve or fifteen feet from the road, and the torch was powerful.

For four or five minutes the stranger made his examination. Then he turned off his torch. "Looks easy," he remarked, "but of course there's the garrison." Once more he turned on his light, to look at his watch. "Can't stop now, or I shall miss the train, and I don't want to have to get a bed at Sprotsfield. A strayed reveler on Christmas night might be too well remembered. Got an address?"

"Care of Mrs. Willnough, Laundress, Inkston."

"Right. Good-night." With a quick turn he was off along the road to Sprotsfield. The Sergeant saw the gleam of his torch once or twice, receding at quite a surprising pace into the distance. Feeling the wad of notes in his pocket—perhaps to make sure that the whole episode had not been a dream—the Sergeant turned back towards Inkston.

After a couple of minutes, a tall figure emerged from the shelter of a high and thick gorse bush just opposite Tower Cottage, on the other side of the road. Captain Alec Naylor had seen the light of the stranger's torch, and, after four years in France, he was well skilled in the art of noiseless approach. But he felt that, for the moment at least, his brain was less agile than his feet. He had been suddenly wrenched out of one set of thoughts into another profoundly different. It was his shadow, together with Cynthia Walford's, that the Sergeant and the stranger had seen on Doctor Mary's blind. After "walking her home," he had—well, just not proposed to Cynthia, restrained more by those scruples of his than by any ungraciousness on the part of the lady. Even his modesty could not blind him to this fact. He was full of pity, of love, of a man's joyous sense of triumph, half wishing that he had made his proposal, half glad that he had not, just because it, and its radiant promise, could still be dangled in the bright vision of the future. He was in the seventh heaven of romance, and his heaven was higher than that which most men reach; it was built on loftier foundations.

Then came the flash of the torch; the high spirits born of one experience sought an outlet in another. "By Jove, I'll track 'em—like old times!" he murmured, with a low light laugh. And, just for fun, he did it, taking to the heath beside the road, twisting his long body in and out amongst gorse, heather, and bracken, very noiselessly, with wonderful dexterity. The light of the lamp was continuous now; the stranger was making his examination. By it Captain Alec guided his steps; and he arrived behind the tall gorse bush opposite Tower Cottage just in time to hear the Sergeant say "Mrs. Willnough, Laundress, Inkston," and to witness the parting of the two companions.

There was very little to go upon there. Why should not one friend give another an address? But the examination? Beaumaroy should surely know of that? It might be nothing, but, on the other hand, it might have a meaning. But the men had gone, had obviously parted for the night. Beaumaroy could be told to-morrow; now he himself could go back to his visions—and so homeward, in happiness, to his bed.

Having reached this sensible conclusion, he was about to turn away from the garden gate which he now stood facing, when he heard the house door softly open and as softly shut. The practice of his profession had given him keen eyes in the dark; he discovered Beaumaroy's tall figure stealing very cautiously down the narrow, flagged path. The next instant the light of another torch flashed out, and this time not in the distance, but full in his own face.

"By God, you, Naylor!" Beaumaroy exclaimed in a voice which was low but full of surprise. "I—I—well, it's rather late—"

Alec Naylor was suddenly struck with the element of humor in the situation. He had been playing detective; apparently he was now the suspected!

"Give me time and I'll explain all," he said, smiling under the dazzling rays of the torch.

Beaumaroy glanced round at the house for a second, pursed up his lips into one of the odd little contortions which he sometimes allowed himself, and said: "Well, then, old chap, come in and have a drink, and do it. For

I'm hanged if I see why you should stand staring into this garden in the middle of the night! With your opportunities I should be better employed on Christmas evening."

"You really want me to come in?" It was now Captain Alec's voice which expressed surprise.

"Why the devil not?" asked Beaumaroy in a tone of frank but friendly impatience.

He turned and led the way into Tower Cottage. Somehow this invitation to enter was the last thing that Captain Alec had expected.

Chapter 8

Captain Alec Raises His Voice

Beaumaroy led the way into the parlor, Captain Alec following. "Well, I thought your old friend didn't care to see strangers," he said, continuing the conversation.

"He was tired and fretful to-night, so I got him to bed, and gave him a soothing draught—one that our friend Dr. Arkroyd sent him. He went off like a lamb, poor old boy. If we don't talk too loud we sha'n't disturb him."

"I can tell you what I have to tell in a few minutes."

"Don't hurry." Beaumaroy was bringing the refreshment he had offered from the sideboard. "I'm feeling lonely to-night, so I—" he smiled—"yielded to the impulse to ask you to come in, Naylor. However, let's have the story by all means."

The surprise—it might almost have been taken for alarm—which he had shown at the first sight of Alec seemed to have given place to a gentle and amiable weariness, which persisted through the recital of the Captain's experiences—how his errand of courtesy, or gallantry, had led to his being on the road across the heath so late at night, and of what he had seen there.

"You copped them properly!" Beaumaroy remarked at the end, with a lazy smile. "One does learn a trick or two in France. You couldn't see their faces, I suppose?"

"No; too dark. I didn't dare show a light, though I had one. Besides, their backs were towards me. One looked tall and thin, the other short and stumpy. But I should never be able to swear to either."

"And they went off in different directions, you say?"

"Yes, the tall one towards Sprotsfield, the short one back towards Inkston."

"Oh, the short stumpy one it was who turned back to Inkston?" Beaumaroy had seated himself on a low three-legged stool, opposite to the big chair where Alec sat, and was smoking his pipe, his hands clasped round his knees. "It doesn't seem to me to come to much, though I'm much obliged to you all the same. The short one's probably a lo-cal, the other a stranger, and the local was probably seeing his friend part of the way home, and incidentally showing him one of the sights of the neighborhood. There are sto-ries about this old den, you know—ancient traditions. It's said to be haunted, and what not."

"Funnily enough, we had the story to-night at dinner, at our house."

"Had you now?" Beaumaroy looked up quickly. "What, all about—"

"Captain Duggle, and the Devil, and the grave, and all that."

"Who told you the story?"

"Old Mr. Penrose. Do you know him? Lives in High Street, near the Irechesters."

"I think I know him by sight. So he entertained you with that old yarn, did he? And that same old yarn prob-ably accounts for the nocturnal examination which you saw going on. It was a little excitement for you, to reward you for your politeness to Miss Walford!"

Alec flushed, but answered frankly: "I needed no reward for that." His feelings got the better of him; he was very full of feelings that night, and wanted to be sympathized with. "Beaumaroy, do you know that girl's story?" Beaumaroy shook his head, and listened to it. Captain Alec ended on his old note: "To think of the scoundrel using the King's uniform like that!"

"Rotten! But, er, don't raise your voice." He pointed to the ceiling, smiling, and went on without further comment on Cynthia's ill-usage. "I suppose you intend to stick to the army, Naylor?"

"Yes, certainly I do."

"I'm discharged. After I came out of hospital they gave me sick leave, and constantly renewed it; and when the armistice came they gave me my discharge. They put it down to my wound, of course, but—well, I gathered the impression that I was considered no great loss." He had finished his pipe, and was now smiling reflectively.

Captain Alec did not smile. Indeed he looked rather pained; he was remembering General Punnit's story: military inefficiency, even military imperfection, was for him no smiling matter. Beaumaroy did not appear to notice his disapproving gravity.

"So I was at a loose end. I had sold up my business in Spain; I was there six or seven years, just as Captain— Captain—? Oh, Cranster, yes!—was in Bogota—when I joined up, and had no particular reason for going back there—and, incidentally, no money to go back with. So I took on this job, which came to me quite accidentally. I went into a Piccadilly bar one evening, and found my old man there, rather excited and declaiming a good deal of rot; seemed to have the war a bit on his brain. They started in to guy him, and I think one or two meant to hustle him, and perhaps take his money off him. I took his part, and there was a bit of a shindy. In the end I saw him home to his lodgings—he had a room in London for the night—and, to cut a long story short, we palled up, and he asked me to come and live with him. So here I am, and with me my Sancho Panza, the worthy ex-Sergeant Hooper. Perhaps I may be forgiven for impliedly comparing myself to Don Quixote, since that gentleman, besides his other characteristics, is generally agreed to have been mad."

"Your Sancho Panza's no beauty," remarked the Captain drily.

"And no saint either. Kicked out of the Service, and done time. That between ourselves."

"Then why the devil do you have the fellow about?"

"Beggars mustn't be choosers. Besides, I've a *penchant* for failures."

That was what General Punnit had said! Alec Naylor grew impatient. "That's the very spirit we have to fight against!" he exclaimed, rather hotly.

"Forgive me, but, please, don't raise your voice."

Alec lowered his voice, for a moment anyhow, but the central article of his creed was assailed, and he grew vehement. "It's fatal; it's at the root of all our troubles. Allow for failures in individuals, and you produce failure all round. It's tenderness to defaulters that wrecks discipline. I would have strict justice, but no mercy, not a shadow of it!"

"But you said that day at your place that the war had made you tender-hearted."

"Yes, I did, and it's true. Is it hard-hearted to refuse to let a slacker cost good men their lives? Much better take his, if it's got to be one or the other."

"A cogent argument. But, my dear Naylor, I wish you wouldn't raise your voice."

"Damn my voice!" said Alec, most vexatiously interrupted just as he had got into his stride. "You say things that I can't and won't let pass, and—"

"I really wouldn't have asked you in, if I'd thought you'd raise your voice."

Alec recollected himself. "My dear fellow, a thousand pardons! I forgot! The old gentleman!"

"Exactly. But I'm afraid the mischief's done. Listen!" Again he pointed to the ceiling, but his eyes set on Captain Alec with a queer, rueful, humorous expression. "I was an ass to ask you in. But I'm no good at it, that's the fact. I'm always giving the show away!" he grumbled, half to himself, but not inaudibly.

Alec stared at him for a moment in puzzle, but the next instant his attention was diverted. Another voice besides his was raised; the sound of it came through the ceiling from the room above; the words were not audible; the volubility of the utterance in itself went far to prevent them from being distinguishable; but the high, vibrant, metallic tones rang through the house. It was a rush of noise, sharp grating noise, without a meaning. The effect was weird, very uncomfortable. Alec Naylor knit his brows, and once gave a little shiver, as he listened. Beaumaroy sat quite still, the expression in his eyes unaltered, or, if altered at all, it grew softer, as though with pity or affection.

"Good God, Beaumaroy, are you keeping a lunatic in this house?" He might raise his voice as loud as he pleased now, it was drowned by that other.

81

"I'm not keeping him, he's keeping me. And, anyhow, his medical adviser tells me there is no reason to suppose that my old friend is not *compos mentis.*"

"Irechester says that?"

"Mr. Saffron's medical attendant is Dr. Arkroyd."

As he spoke the noise from above suddenly ceased. Since neither of the men in the parlor spoke, there ensued a minute of what seemed intense silence; it was such a change.

Then came a still small sound, a creaking of wood from overhead.

"I think you'd better go, Naylor, if you don't mind. After a performance of that kind he generally comes and tells me about it. And he may be, I don't know at all for certain, annoyed to find you here."

Alec Naylor got up from the big chair, but it was not to take his departure.

"I want to see him, Beaumaroy," he said brusquely and rather authoritatively.

Beaumaroy raised his brows. "I won't take you to his room, or let you go there if I can help it. But if he comes down, well, you can stay and see him. It may get me into a scrape, but that doesn't matter much."

"My point of view is—"

"My dear fellow, I know your point of view perfectly. It is that you are personally responsible for the universe, apparently just because you wear a uniform."

No other sound had come from above or from the stairs, but the door now opened suddenly, and Mr. Saffron stood on the threshold. He wore slippers, a pair of checked trousers, and his bedroom jacket of pale blue; in addition, the gray shawl, which he wore on his walks, was again swathed closely round him. Only his right arm was free from it; in his hand was a silver bedroom candlestick. From his pale face and under his snowy hair his blue eyes gleamed brightly. As Alec first caught sight of him, he was smiling happily, and he called out triumphantly: "That was a good one! That went well, Hector!"

Then he saw Alec's tall figure by the fire. He grew grave, closed the door carefully, and advanced to the table, on which he set down the candlestick. After a momentary look at Alec, he turned his gaze inquiringly towards Beaumaroy.

"I'm afraid we're keeping it up rather late, sir," said the latter in a tone of respectful yet easy apology, "but I took an airing in the road after you went to bed, and there I found my friend here on his way home; and since it was Christmas—"

Mr. Saffron bowed his head in acquiescence; he showed no sign of anger. "Present your friend to me, Hector," he requested, or ordered, gravely.

"Captain Naylor, sir, Distinguished Service Order; Duffshire Fusiliers."

The Captain was in uniform and, during his talk with Beaumaroy, had not thought of taking off his cap. Thus he came to the salute instinctively. The old man bowed with reserved dignity; in spite of his queer get-up he bore himself well; the tall handsome Captain did not seem to efface or outclass him.

"Captain Naylor has distinguished himself highly in the war, sir," Beaumaroy continued.

"I am very glad to make the acquaintance of any officer who has distinguished himself in the service of his country." Then his tone became easier and more familiar.

"Don't let me disturb you, gentlemen. My business with you, Hector, will wait. I have finished my work, and can rest with a clear conscience."

"Couldn't we persuade you to stay a few minutes with us, and join us in a whisky-and-soda?"

"Yes, by all means, Hector. But no whisky. Give me a glass of my own wine; I see a bottle on the sideboard."

He came round the table and sat down in the big chair. "Pray seat yourself, Captain," he said, waving his hand towards the stool which Beaumaroy had lately occupied.

The Captain obeyed the gesture, but his huge frame looked awkward on the low seat; he felt aware of it, then aware of the cap on his head; he snatched it off hastily, and twiddled it between his fingers. Mr. Saffron, high up in the great chair, sitting erect, seemed now actually to dominate the scene—Beaumaroy standing by, with an arm on the back of the chair, holding a tall glass full of the golden wine ready to Mr. Saffron's command; the old man reached up his thin right hand, took it, and sipped with evident pleasure.

Alec Naylor was embarrassed; he sat in silence. But Beaumaroy seemed quite at his ease. He began with a statement which was, in its literal form, no falsehood; but that was about all that could be said for it on the score of veracity. "Before you came in, sir, we were just speaking of uniforms. Do you remember seeing our blue Air Force uniform when we were in town last week? I remember that you expressed approval of it."

In any case the topic was very successful. Mr. Saffron embraced it with eagerness; with much animation he discussed the merits, whether practical or decorative, of various uniforms—field-gray, khaki, horizon blue, Air Force blue, and a dozen others worn by various armies, corps, and services. Alec was something of an enthusiast in this line too; he soon forgot his embarrassment, and joined in the conversation freely, though with a due respect to the obvious thoroughness of Mr. Saffron's information. Watching the pair with an amused smile, Beaumaroy contented himself with putting in, here and there, what may be called a conjunctive observation—just enough to give the topic a new start.

After a quarter of an hour of this pleasant conversation, for such all three seemed to find it, Mr. Saffron finished his wine, handed the glass to Beaumaroy, and took a cordial leave of Alec Naylor. "It's time for me to be in bed, but don't hurry away, Captain. You won't disturb me, I'm a good sleeper. Good-bye. I sha'n't want you any more to-night, Hector."

Beaumaroy handed him his candle again, and held the door open for him as he went out.

Alec Naylor clapped his cap back on his head. "I'm off too," he said abruptly.

"Well, you insisted on seeing him, and you've seen him. What about it now?" asked Beaumaroy.

Alec eyed him with a puzzled baffled suspicion. "You switched him on to that subject on purpose, and by means of something uncommon like a lie."

"A little artifice! I knew it would interest you, and it's quite one of his hobbies. I don't know much about his past life, but I think he must have had something to do with military tailoring. A designer at the War Office, perhaps." Beaumaroy gave a low laugh, rather mocking and malicious. "Still, that doesn't prove a man mad, does it? Perhaps it ought to, but in general opinion it doesn't, any more than reciting poetry in bed does."

"Do you mean to tell me that he was reciting poetry when—"

"Well, it couldn't have sounded worse if he had been, could it?"

Now he was openly laughing at the Captain's angry bewilderment. He knew that Alec Naylor did not believe a word of what he was saying or suggesting; but yet Alec could not pass his guard, nor wing a shaft between the joints of his harness. If he got into difficulties through heedlessness, at least he made a good shot at getting out of them again by his dexterity. Only, of course, suspicion remains suspicion, even though it be, for the moment, baffled. And it could not be denied that suspicions were piling up—Captain Alec, Irechester, even, on one little point, Doctor Mary! And possibly those two fellows outside—one of them short and stumpy—had their suspicions too, though these might be directed to another point. He gave one of his little shrugs as he followed the silent Captain to the garden gate.

"Good-night. Thanks again. And I hope we shall meet soon," he said cheerily.

Alec gave him a brief "Good-night" and a particularly formal military salute.

Chapter 9

Doctor Mary's Ultimatum

Even Captain Alec was not superior to the foibles which beset humanity. If it had been his conception of duty which impelled him to take a high line with Beaumaroy, there was now in his feelings, although he did not realize the fact, an alloy of less precious metal. He had demanded an ordeal, a test—that he should see Mr. Saffron and judge for himself. The test had been accepted; he had been worsted in it. His suspicions were not laid to rest—far from it; but they were left unjustified and unconfirmed. He had nothing to go upon, nothing to show. He had been baffled, and, moreover, bantered and almost openly ridiculed. In fact, Beaumaroy had been too many for him, the subtle rogue!

This conception of the case colored his looks and pointed his words when Tower Cottage and its occupants were referred to, and most markedly when he spoke of them to Cynthia Walford; for in talking to her he naturally allowed himself greater freedom than he did with others; talking to her had become like talking to himself, so completely did she give him back what he bestowed on her, and re-echo to his mind its own voice. Such perfect sympathy induces a free outpouring of inner thoughts, and reinforces the opinions of which it so unreservedly approves.

Cynthia did more than elicit and reinforce Captain Alec's opinion; she also disseminated it—at Old Place, at the Irechesters', at Doctor Mary's, through all the little circle in which she was now a constant and a favorite figure. In the light of her experience of men, so limited and so sharply contrasted, she made a simple classification of them; they were Cransters or Alecs; and each class acted after its kind. Plainly Beaumaroy was not an Alec; therefore he was Cranster, and Cranster-like actions were to be expected from him, of such special description as his circumstances and temptations might dictate.

She poured this simple philosophy into Doctor Mary's ears, vouching Alec's authority for its application to Beaumaroy. The theory was too simple for Mary, whose profession had shown her at all events something of the complexity of human nature; and she was no infallibilist; she would bow unquestioningly to no man's authority, not even to Alec's, much as she liked and admired him. There was even a streak of contrariness in her; what she might have said to herself she was prone to criticize or contradict, if it were too confidently or urgently pressed on her by another; perhaps, too, Cynthia's claim to be the Captain's mouthpiece stirred up in her a latent resentment; it was not to be called a jealousy; it was rather an amused irritation at both the divinity and his worshiper. His worshipers can sometimes make a divinity look foolish.

Her own interview with Beaumaroy at the Cottage had left her puzzled, distrustful—and attracted. She suspected him vaguely of wanting to use her for some purpose of his own; in spite of the swift plausibility of his explanation, she was nearly certain that he had lied to her about the combination knife-and-fork. Yet his account of his own position in regard to Mr. Saffron had sounded remarkably candid, and the more so because he made no pretensions to an exalted attitude. It had been left to her to define the standard of sensitive honor; his had been rather that of safety or, at the best, that of what the world would think, or even of what the hated cousins might attempt to prove. But there again she was distrustful, both of him and of her own judgment. He might be—it seemed likely—one of those men who conceal the good as well as the bad in themselves, one of the morally shy men. Or again, perhaps, one of the morally diffident, who shrink from arrogating to themselves high standards because they fear for their own virtue if it be put to the test, and cling to the power of saying, later on, "Well, I told you not to expect too much from me!" Such various types of men exist, and they do not fall readily into either of Cynthia's two classes; they are neither Cransters nor Alecs; certainly not in thought, probably not in conduct. He had said at Old Place, the first time that she met him, that the war had destroyed all his scruples. That might be true; but it was hardly the remark of a man naturally unscrupulous.

She met him one day at Old Place about a week after Christmas. The Captain was not there; he was at her own house, with Cynthia. With the rest of the family Beaumaroy was at his best; gaily respectful to Mrs. Naylor, merry with Gertie, exchanging cut and thrust with old Mr. Naylor, easy and cordial towards herself. Certainly an attractive human being and a charming companion, pre-eminently natural. "One talks of taking people as one finds them," old Naylor said to her when they were left alone together for a few minutes by the fire, while the others chatted by the window. "That fellow takes himself as he finds himself! Not as a pattern, a failure, or a problem, but just as a fact—a psychological fact."

"That rather shuts out effort, doesn't it? Well, I mean—"

"Strivings?" Mr. Naylor smiled. "Yes, it does. On the other hand, it gives such free play. That's what makes him interesting, makes you think about him." He laughed. "Oh, I dare say the surroundings help too—we're all rather children—old Saffron, and the Devil, and Captain Duggle, and the rest of it! The brain isn't overworked down here; we like to find an outlet."

"That means you think there's nothing in it really?"

"In what?" retorted old Naylor briskly.

But Mary was equal to him. "My lips are sealed professionally," she smiled. "But hasn't your son said anything?"

"Admirable woman! Yes, Alec has said a few things; and the young lady gives it us, too. For my part, I think Beaumaroy's just drifting. He'll take the gifts of fortune if they come, but I don't think there's much deliberate design about it. Ah, now you're smiling in a superior way, Doctor Mary! I charge you with secret knowledge. Or are you puffed up by having superseded Irechester?"

"I was never so distressed and—well, embarrassed at anything in my life."

"Well, that, if you ask me, does look a bit queer. Sort of fits in with Alec's theory."

Mary's discretion gave way a little. "Or with Mr. Beaumaroy's? Which is that I'm a fool, I think."

"And that Irechester isn't?" His eyes twinkled in good-humored malice. "Talking of what this and that person thinks of himself and of others, Irechester thinks himself something of an alienist."

Her eyes grew suddenly alert. "He's never talked to me on that subject."

"Perhaps he doesn't think it's one of yours. Perhaps your studies haven't lain that way? After all, no medical man can study everything!"

"Don't be naughty, Mr. Naylor" said Doctor Mary.

"He tells me that, in cases where the condition—the condition I think he called it—is in doubt, he fixes his attention on the eyes and the voice. He couldn't give me any very clear description of what he found in the eyes. I couldn't quite make out, anyhow, what he meant, unless it was a sort of meaninglessness, a want of what you might call intellectual focus. Do you follow me?"

"Yes, I think I know what you mean."

"But with regard to the voice I distinctly remember that he used the word 'metallic.'"

"Why, that's the word Cynthia used—"

"I dare say it is. It's the word Alec used in describing the voice in which old Mr. Saffron recited his poem, or whatever it was, in bed."

"But I've talked to Mr. Saffron; his voice isn't like that; it's a little high, but full and rather melodious."

"Oh, well then—" He spread out his hands, as though acknowledging a check. "Still, the voice described as metallic seems to have been Mr. Saffron's; at a certain moment at least. As a merely medical question of some interest, I wonder if such a symptom or sign of—er—irritability could be intermittent, coming and going with the—er—fits! Irechester didn't say anything on that point. Have you any opinion?"

"None. I don't know. I should like to ask Dr. Irechester." Then, with a sudden smile, she amended, "No, I shouldn't!"

"And why not, pray? Professional etiquette?"

"No, pride. Dr. Irechester laughed at me. I think I see why now; and perhaps why Mr. Beaumaroy—" She broke off abruptly, the slightest gesture of her hand warning Naylor also to be silent.

Having said good-bye to his friends by the window, Beaumaroy was sauntering across the room to pay the like courtesy to herself and Naylor. Mary rose to her feet; there was an air of decision about her, and she addressed Beaumaroy almost before he was within speaking distance as it is generally reckoned in society.

"If you're going home, Mr. Beaumaroy, shall we walk together? It's time I was off, too."

Beaumaroy looked a little surprised, but undoubtedly pleased. "Well, now, what a delightful way of prolonging a delightful visit. I'm truly grateful, Dr. Arkroyd."

"Oh, you needn't be!" said Mary with a little toss of her head.

Naylor watched them with amusement. "He'll catch it on that walk!" he was thinking. "She's going to let him have it! I wish I could be there to hear." He spoke to them openly: "I'm sorry you must both go, but, since you must, go together. Your walk will be much pleasanter."

Mary understood him well enough, and gave him a flash from her eyes. But Beaumaroy's face betrayed nothing, as he murmured politely: "To me, at all events, Mr. Naylor."

Naylor was not wrong as to Mary's mood and purpose. But she did not find it easy to begin. Pretty quick at a retort herself, she could often foresee the retorts open to her interlocutor. Beaumaroy had provided himself with plenty: the old man's whim; the access to the old man so willingly allowed, not only to her but to Captain Alec; his own candor carried to the verge of self-betrayal. Oh, he would be full of retorts, supple and dexterous ones! As this hostile accusation passed through her mind, she awoke to the fact that she was, at the same moment, regarding his profile (he, too, was silent, no doubt lying in wait to trip up her opening!) with interest, even with some approval. He seemed to feel her glance, for he turned towards her quickly—so quickly that she had no time to turn her eyes away.

"Doctor Mary"—the familiar mode of address habitually used at the house which they had just left seemed to slip out without his consciousness of it—"You've got something against me; I know you have! I'm sensitive that way, though not, perhaps, in another. Now, out with it!"

"You'd silence me with a clever answer. I think that you sometimes make the mistake of supposing that to be silenced is the same thing as being convinced. You silenced Captain Naylor—oh, I don't mean you've prevented him from talking!—I mean you confuted him, you put him in the wrong, but you certainly didn't convince him."

"Of what?" he asked in a tone of surprise.

"You know that. Let us suppose his idea was all nonsense; yet your immediate object was to put it out of his head." She suddenly added, "I think your last question was a diplomatic blunder, Mr. Beaumaroy. You must have known what I meant. What was the good of pretending not to?"

Beaumaroy stopped still in the road for a moment, looking at her with a rueful amusement. "You're not so easily silenced, after all!" he said, starting to walk on again.

"You encourage me." To tell the truth, Mary was not only encouraged, she was pleased by the hit she had scored, and flattered by his acknowledgment of it. "Well, then, I'll put another point. You needn't answer if you don't like."

"I shall answer if I can, depend on it!" He laughed, and Mary, for a brief instant, joined in his laugh. His sudden lapses into candor seemed somehow to put the serious hostile questioner ridiculously in the wrong. Could a man like that really have anything to conceal?

But she held to her purpose. "You're a friendly sort of man, you offer and accept attentions and kindnesses, you're not stand-offish, or haughty, or sulky; you make friends easily, especially, perhaps, with women; they like you, and like to be pleasant and kind to you. There are men—patients, I mean—very hard to deal with; men who resent being ill, resent having to have things done to them and for them, who especially resent the services of women, even of nurses—I mean in quite indifferent things, not merely in things where a man may naturally shrink from their help. Well, you don't seem that sort of man in the least." She looked at him, as she ended this appreciation of him, as though she expected an answer or a comment. Beaumaroy made neither; he walked on, not even looking at her.

"And you can't have been troubled long with that wound. It evidently healed up quickly and sweetly."

Beaumaroy looked for an instant at his maimed hand with a critical air; but he was still silent.

"So that I wonder you didn't do as most patients do—let the nurse, or, if you were still disabled after you came out, a friend or somebody, cut up your food for you without providing yourself with that implement." He turned his head quickly towards her. "And if you ask me what implement I mean, I shall answer—the one you tried to snatch from the sideboard at Tower Cottage before I could see it."

It was a direct challenge; she charged him with a lie. Beaumaroy's face assumed a really troubled expression, a thing rare for it to do. Yet it was not an ashamed or abashed expression; it just seemed to recognize that a troublesome difficulty had arisen. He set a slower pace and prodded the road with his stick. Mary pushed her advantage. "Your—your improvization didn't satisfy me at the time, and the more I've thought over it, the less have I found it convincing."

He stopped again, turning round to her. He slapped his left hand against the side of his leg. "Well, there it is, Doctor Mary! You must make what you can of it."

It was complete surrender as to the combination knife-and-fork. He was beaten, on that point at least, and owned it. His lie was found out. "It's dashed difficult always to remember that you're a doctor," he broke out the next minute.

Mary could not help laughing; but her eyes were still keen and challenging as she said, "Perhaps you'd better change your doctor again, Mr. Beaumaroy. You haven't found one stupid enough!"

Again Beaumaroy had no defense; his nonplussed air confessed that maneuver, too. Mary dropped her rallying tone and went on gravely: "Unless I'm treated with confidence and sincerity, I can't continue to attend Mr. Saffron."

"That's your ultimatum, is it, Doctor Mary?"

She nodded sharply and decisively. Beaumaroy meditated for a few seconds. Then he shook his head regretfully. "It's no use. I daren't trust you," he said.

Mary laughed again, this time in amazed resentment of his impudence. "You can't trust me! I think it's the other way round. It seems to me that the boot's on the other leg."

"Not as I see it." Then he smiled slowly, as it were tentatively. "Or would you—I wonder if you could—possibly—well, stand in with me?"

"Are you offering me a—a partnership?" she asked indignantly.

He raised his hand in a seeming protest, and spoke now hastily and in some confusion. "Not as you understand it. I mean, as you probably understand it, from what I said to you that night at the Cottage. There are features in the—well, there are things that I admit have—have passed through my mind, without being what you'd call settled. Oh, yes, without being in the least settled. Well, for the sake of your help and—er—co-operation, those—those features could be dropped. And then perhaps—if only your—your rules and etiquette—"

Mary scornfully cut short his embarrassed pleadings. "There's a good deal more than rules and etiquette involved. It seems to me that it's a matter of common honesty rather than of rules and etiquette—"

"Yes, but you don't understand—"

She cut him short again. "Mr. Beaumaroy, after this, after your suggestion and all the rest of it, there must be an end of all relations between us—professionally and, so far as possible, socially too, please. I don't want to be self-righteous, but I feel bound to say that you have misunderstood my character."

Her voice quivered at the end, and almost broke. She was full of a grieved indignation.

They had come opposite the cottage now. Beaumaroy stopped, and stood facing her. Though dusk had fallen, it was a clear evening; she could see his face plainly; obviously he was in deep distress. "I wouldn't have offended you for the world. I—I like you far too much, Doctor Mary."

"You imputed your own standards to me. That's all there is about it, I suppose," she said in a scornful sadness. He looked very miserable. Compassion, and the old odd attraction which he had for her, stirred in her mind. Her voice grew soft, and she held out her hand. "I'm sorry too, very sorry, that it should have to be good-bye between us."

Beaumaroy did not take her proffered hand, or even seem to notice it. He stood quite still.

"I'm damned if I know what I'm to do now!"

Close on the heels of his despairing confession of helplessness—for such it undoubtedly seemed to me—came the noise of an opening door, a light from the inside of the Cottage, a patter of quick-moving feet on the flagged path that led to the garden gate. The next moment Mary saw the figure of Mr. Saffron, in his old gray shawl, standing at the gate. He was waving his right arm in an excited way, and his hand held a large sheet of paper.

"Hector! Hector, my dear, dear boy! The news has come at last. You can be off tomorrow!"

Beaumaroy started violently, glanced at his old friend's strange figure, glanced once, too, at Mary; the expression of utter despair which his face had worn seemed modified into one of humorous bewilderment.

"Yes, yes, you can start tomorrow for Morocco, my dear boy!" cried old Mr. Saffron.

Beaumaroy lifted his hat to her, cried, "I'm coming, sir!" turned on his heel, and strode quickly up to Mr. Saffron. She watched him open the gate and take the old gentleman by the arm; she heard the murmur of his voice speaking soft accents as the pair walked up the path together. They passed into the house, and the door was shut.

Mary stood where she was for a moment, then moved slowly, hesitatingly, yet as though under a lure which she could not resist. Just outside the gate lay something that gleamed white through the darkness. It was the sheet of paper. Mr. Saffron had dropped it in his excitement, and Beaumaroy had not noticed.

Mary stole forward and picked it up stealthily; she was incapable of resisting her curiosity or even of stopping to think about her action. She held it up to what light there was, and strained her eyes to examine it. So far as she could see, it was covered with dots, dashes, lines, queerly drawn geometrical figures—a mass of meaningless hieroglyphics. She dropped it again where she had found it, and made off home with guilty swiftness.

Yes, there had been, this time, a distinctly metallic ring in old Mr. Saffron's voice.

Chapter 10

The Magical Word Morocco!

When Mary arrived home, she found Cynthia and Captain Alec still in possession of the drawing-room; their manner accused her legitimate entry into the room of being an outrageous intrusion. She took no heed of that, and indeed little heed of them. To tell the truth, she was ashamed to confess, but it was the truth, she felt rather tired of them that evening. Their affair deserved every laudatory epithet, except that of interesting; so she declared peevishly within herself as she tried to join in conversation with them. It was no use. They talked on, and in justice to them it may be urged that they were fully as bored with Mary as she was with them; so naturally their talents did not shine their brightest. But they had plenty to say to one another, and dutifully threw in a question or a reference to Mary every now and then. Sitting apart at the other end of the long low room—it ran through the whole depth of her old-fashioned dwelling—she barely heeded and barely answered. They smiled at one another and were glad.

She was very tired; her feelings were wounded, her nerves on edge; she could not even attempt any cool train of reasoning. The outcome of her talk with Beaumaroy filled her mind rather than the matter of it; and, more even than that, the figure of the man seemed to be with her, almost to stand before her, with his queer alternations of despair and mirth, of defiance and pleading, of derision and alarm. One moment she was intensely irritated with him; in the next she half forgave the plaintive image which the fancy of her mind conjured up before her eyes.

Her eyes closed—she was so very tired, the fight had taken it out of her! To have to do things like that was an odious necessity, which had never befallen her before. That man had done—well, Captain Alec was quite right about him! Yet still the shadowy image, though thus reproached, did not depart; it was smiling at her now with its old mockery—the kindly mockery which his face wore before they quarrelled, and before its light was quenched in that forlorn bewilderment. And it seemed as though the image began to say some words to her, disconnected words, not making a sentence, but yet having for the image a pregnant meaning, and seeming to her—though vaguely and very dimly—to be the key to what she had to understand. She was stupid not to understand words so full of meaning—just as stupid as Beaumaroy had thought.

Then Doctor Mary fell asleep, sound asleep; she had been very near it for the last ten minutes.

Captain Alec and Cynthia were in two chairs, close side by side, in front of the fire. Once Cynthia glanced over her shoulder; the Captain had glanced over his in the same direction already. One of his hands held one of Cynthia's. It was well to be sure that Mary was asleep, really asleep.

She had gone to sleep on the name of Beaumaroy; on it she awoke. It came from Captain Alec's lips. He was standing on the hearthrug with his arm round Cynthia's waist, and his other hand raising one of hers to his lips. He looked admirably handsome—strong, protecting, devoted. And Cynthia, in her fragile appealing prettiness, was a delicious foil, a perfect complement to the picture. But now, under stress of emotion—small blame to a man who was making a vow of eternal fidelity!—under stress of emotion, as, on a previous occasion, under that of indignation, the Captain had raised his voice!

"Yes, against all the scoundrels in the world, whether they're called Cranster or Beaumaroy!" he said.

Mary's eyes opened. She sat up. "Cranster and Beaumaroy?" They were the words which her ears had caught. "What in the world has Mr. Beaumaroy to do with—" But she broke off, as she saw the couple by the fire. "But what are you two doing?"

Cynthia broke away from her lover, and ran to her friend with joyous avowals.

"I must have been sound asleep," cried Mary, kissing her. Alec had followed across the room and now stood close by her. She looked up at him. "Oh, I see! She's to be safe now from such people?" On this particular occasion Mary's look at the Captain was not admiring; it was a little scornful.

"That's the idea," agreed the happy Alec. "Another idea is that I trot you both over in the car to Old Place—to break the news and have dinner."

"Splendid!" cried Cynthia. "Do come, Mary!"

Mary shook her head. "No; you go, you two," she said. "I'm tired, and I want to think." She passed her hand across her eyes. She seemed to wipe away the mists of sleep. Her face suddenly grew animated and exultant. "No, I don't want to think! I know!" she exclaimed emphatically.

"Mary dear, are you still asleep? Are you talking in your sleep?"

"The keyword! It came to me, somehow, in my sleep. The keyword—Morocco!"

"What the deuce has Morocco—" Captain Alec began, with justifiable impatience.

"Ah, you never heard that, and, dear Captain Alec, you wouldn't have understood it if you had. You thought he was reciting poems. What he was really doing—"

"Look here, Doctor Mary, I've just been accepted by Cynthia, and I'm going to take her to my mother and father. Can you get your mind on to that?" He looked at her curiously, not at all understanding her excitement, perhaps resenting the obvious fact that his Cynthia's happiness was not foremost in her friend's mind.

With a great effort Mary brought herself down to the earth—to the earth of romantic love from the heaven of professional triumph. True, the latter was hers, the former somebody else's. "I do beg your pardon. I do indeed. And do let me kiss you again, Cynthia darling—and you, dear Captain Alec, just once! And then you shall go off to dinner." She laughed excitedly. "Yes, I'm going to push you out."

"Let's go, Alec," said Cynthia, not unkindly, yet just a little pettishly. The great moment of her life—surely as great a moment as there had ever been in anybody's life—had hardly earned adequate recognition from Mary. As usual, her feelings and Alec's were at one. Before they passed to other and more important matters, when they drove off in the car she said to Alec, "It seems to me that Mary's strangely interested in that Mr. Beaumaroy. Had she been dreaming of him, Alec?"

"Looks like it! And why the devil Morocco?" His intellect baffled, Captain Alec took refuge in his affections.

Left alone, and so thankful for it, Doctor Mary did not attempt to sit still. She walked up and down, she roved here and there, smoking any quantity of cigarettes; she would certainly have forbidden such excess to a patient. The keyword; its significance had seemed to come to her in her sleep. Something in that subconsciousness theory? The word explained, linked up, gave significance—that magical word Morocco!

Yes, they fell into place now, the things that had been so puzzling, and that looked now so obviously suggestive. Even one thing which she had thought nothing about, which had not struck her as having any significance, now took on its meaning—the gray shawl which the old gentleman so constantly wore swathed round his body, enveloping the whole of it except his right arm. Did he wear the shawl while he took his meals? Doctor Mary could not tell as to that. Perhaps he did not; at his meals only Beaumaroy, and perhaps their servant, would be present. But he seemed to wear it whenever he went abroad, whenever he was exposed to the scrutiny of strangers. That indicated secretiveness, perhaps fear, the apprehension of something. The caution bred by that might give way under the influence of great cerebral excitement. Unquestionably Mr. Saffron had been very excited when he waved the sheet of hieroglyphics and shouted to Beaumaroy about Morocco. But whether he wore the shawl or not in the safe privacy of Tower Cottage, whatever might be the truth about that—perhaps he varied his practice according to his condition—on one thing Doctor Mary would stake her life; he used the combination knife-and-fork!

For it was over that implement that Beaumaroy had tripped up. It ought to have been hidden before she was admitted to the cottage. Somebody had been careless, somebody had blundered—whether Beaumaroy himself or his servant was immaterial. Beaumaroy had lied, readily and ingeniously, but not quite readily enough. The dart of his hand had betrayed him; that, and a look in his eyes, a tell-tale mirth which had seemed to mock both her and himself, and had made his ingenious lie even at the moment unconvincing. Yes, whether Mr. Saffron wore the shawl or not, he certainly used the combination table implement!

And the "poems?" The poems which Mr. Saffron recited to himself in bed, and which he had said, in Captain Alec's hearing, were good and "went well." It was Beaumaroy, of course, who had called them poems; the Captain had merely repeated the description. But with her newly found insight Doctor Mary knew better. What Mr. Saffron declaimed in that vibrating, metallic voice, were not poems, but—speeches!

And "Morocco" itself! To anybody who remembered history for a few years back, even with the general memory of the man in the street, to anybody who had read the controversies about the war, Morocco brought not puzzle, but enlightenment. For had not Morocco been really the starting point of the Years of Crisis—those years intermittent in excitement, but constant in anxiety? Beaumaroy was to start tomorrow for Morocco—on the strength of the hieroglyphics! Perhaps he was to go on from Morocco to Libya; perhaps he was to raise the Senussi (Mary had followed the history of the war), to make his appearance at Cairo, Jerusalem, Bagdad! He was to be a forerunner, was Mr. Beaumaroy. Mr. Saffron, his august master, would follow in due course! With a sardonic smile she wondered how the ingenious man would get out of starting for Morocco; perhaps he would not succeed in obtaining a passport, or, that excuse failing, in eluding the vigilance of the British authorities. Or some more hieroglyphics might come, carrying another message, postponing his start, saying that the propitious moment had not yet arrived after all. There were several devices open to ingenuity; many ways in which Beaumaroy might protract a situation not so bad for him even as it stood, and quite rich in possibilities. Her acid smile was turned against herself when she remembered that she had been fool enough to talk to Beaumaroy about sensitive honor!

Well, never mind Mr. Beaumaroy! The case as to Mr. Saffron stood pretty plain. It was queer and pitiful, but by no means unprecedented. She might be not much of an alienist, as Dr. Irechester had been kind enough to suggest to Mr. Naylor, but she had seen such cases herself—even stranger ones, where even higher Powers suffered impersonation, with effects still more tragically absurd to onlookers. And she remembered reading somewhere—was it in Maudslay—that in the days of Napoleon, when princes and kings were as ninepins to be set up and knocked down at the tyrant's pleasure, the asylums of France were full of such great folk? Potentates there galore! If she had Mr. Saffron's "record" before her, she would expect to read of a vain ostentatious man, ambitious in his own small way; the little plant of these qualities would, given a morbid physical condition, develop into the fantastic growth of delusion which she had now diagnosed in the case of Mr. Saffron—diagnosed with the assistance of some lucky accidents!

But what was her duty now—the duty of Dr. Mary Arkroyd, a duly qualified, accredited, responsible medical practitioner? With a slight shock to her self-esteem she was obliged to confess that she had only the haziest idea. Had not people who kept a lunatic to be licensed or something? Or did that apply only to lunatics in the plural? And did Beaumaroy keep Mr. Saffron within the meaning of whatever the law might be? But at any rate she must do something; the state of things at Tower Cottage could not go on as it was. The law of the land—whatever it was—must be observed, Beaumaroy must be foiled, and poor old Mr. Saffron taken proper care of. The course of her meditations was hardly interrupted by the episode of her light evening meal; she was back in her drawing-room by half past eight, her mind engrossed with the matter still.

It was a little after nine when there was a ring at the hall door. Not the lovers back so early? She heard a man's voice in the hall. The next moment Beaumaroy was shown in, and the door shut behind him. He stood still by it, making no motion to advance towards her. He was breathing quickly, and she noticed beads of perspiration on his forehead. She had sprung to her feet at the sight of him and faced him with indignation.

"You have no right to come here, Mr. Beaumaroy, after what passed between us this afternoon."

"Besides being, as you saw yourself, very excited, my poor old friend isn't at all well tonight."

"I'm very sorry; but I'm no longer Mr. Saffron's medical attendant. If I declined to be this afternoon, I decline ten times more tonight."

"For all I know, he's very ill indeed, Dr. Arkroyd." Beaumaroy's manner was very quiet, restrained, and formal.

"I have come to a clear conclusion about Mr. Saffron's case since I left you."

"I thought you might. I suppose 'Morocco' put you on the scent? And I suppose, too, that you looked at that wretched bit of paper?"

"I—I thought of it—" Here Mary was slightly embarrassed.

"You'd have been more than human if you hadn't. I was out again after it in five minutes—as soon as I missed it; you'd gone, but I concluded you'd seen it. He scribbles dozens like that."

"You seem to admit my conclusion about his mental condition," she observed stiffly.

"I always admit when I cease to be able to deny. But don't let's stand here talking. Really, for all I know, he may be dying. His heart seems to me very bad."

"Go and ask Dr. Irechester."

"He dreads Irechester. I believe the sight of Irechester might finish him. You must come."

"I can't—for the reasons I've told you."

"Why? My misdeeds? Or your rules and regulations? My God, how I hate rules and regulations! Which of them is it that is perhaps to cost the old man his life?"

Mary could not resist the appeal; that could hardly be her duty, and certainly was not her inclination. Her grievance was not against poor old Mr. Saffron, with his pitiful delusion of greatness, of a greatness, too, which now had suffered an eclipse almost as tragical as that which had befallen his own reason. What an irony in his mad aping of it now!

"I will come, Mr. Beaumaroy, on condition that you give me candidly and truthfully all the information which, as Mr. Saffron's medical attendant, I am entitled to ask."

"I'll tell you all I know about him, and about myself, too."

"Your affairs and—er—position matter to me only so far as they bear on Mr. Saffron."

"So be it. Only come quickly; and bring some of your things that may help a man with a bad heart."

Mary left him, went to her surgery, and was quickly back with her bag. "I'll get out the car."

"It'll take a little longer, I know, but do you mind if we walk? Cars always alarm him. He thinks that they come to take him away. Every car that passes vexes him; he looks to see if it will stop. And when yours does—" He ended with a shrug.

For the first time Mary's feelings took on a keen edge of pity. Poor old gentleman! Fancy his living like that! And cars, military cars, too, had been so common on the road across the heath.

"I understand. Let us go at once. You walked yourself, I suppose?"

"Ran," said Beaumaroy, and, with the first sign of a smile, wiped the sweat from his brow with the back of his hand.

"I'm ready, Mr. Beaumaroy," said Doctor Mary.

They walked along together in silence for fully half the way. Then Beaumaroy spoke. "He was extremely excited—at his worst—when he and I went into the cottage. I had to humor him in every way; it was the only thing to do. That was followed by great fatigue, a sort of collapse. I persuaded him to go to bed. I hope we shall find him there, but I don't know. He would let me go only on condition that I left the door of the Tower unlocked, so that he could go in there if he wanted to. If he has, I'm afraid that you may see something—well, something rather bizarre, Dr. Arkroyd."

"That's all in the course of my profession."

Silence fell on them again, till the outline of cottage and Tower came into view through the darkness. Beaumaroy spoke only once again before they reached the garden gate.

"If he should happen to be calmer now, I hope you will not consider it necessary to tell him that you suspect anything unusual."

"He is secretive?"

"He lives in terror."

"Of what?"

"Of being shut up. May I lead the way in, Dr. Arkroyd?"

They entered the cottage, and Beaumaroy shut the door. A lamp was burning dimly in the passage. He turned it up. "Would you kindly wait here one minute?" Receiving her nod of acquiescence, he stepped softly up the stairs, and she heard him open a door above; she knew it was that of Mr. Saffron's bedroom, where she had visited the old man. She waited, now with a sudden sense of suspense. It was very quiet in the cottage.

Beaumaroy was down again in a minute.

"It is as I feared," he said quietly. "He has got up again, and gone into the Tower. Shall I try and get him out, or will you—"

"I will go in with you, of course, Mr. Beaumaroy."

His old mirthful, yet rueful, smile came on his lips— just for a moment. Then he was grave and formal again. "This way, then, if you please, Dr. Arkroyd," he said deferentially.

Chapter 11

The Car Behind the Trees

Mr. Percy Bennett, that gentlemanly stranger, was an enemy to delay; both constitutionally and owing to experience, averse from dallying with fortune; to him a bird in his hand was worth a whole aviary on his neighbor's unrifled premises. He thought that Beaumaroy might levant with the treasure; at any moment that unwelcome, though not unfamiliar, tap on the shoulder, with the words (gratifying under quite other circumstances and from quite different lips) "I want you," might incapacitate him from prosecuting his enterprise (he expressed this idea in more homely idiom—less Latinized was his language, metaphorical indeed, yet terse); finally he had that healthy distrust of his accomplices which is essential to success in a career of crime; he thought that Sergeant Hooper might not deliver the goods!

Sergeant Hooper demurred; he deprecated inconsiderate haste? let the opportunity be chosen. He had served under Mr. Beaumaroy in France, and (whatever faults Major-General Punnit might find with that officer) preferred that he should be off the premises at the moment when Mr. Bennett and he himself made unauthorized entry thereon. "He's a hot 'un in a scrap," said the Sergeant, sitting in a public house at Sprotsfield on Boxing Day evening, Mr. Bennett and sundry other excursionists from London being present.

"My chauffeur will settle him," said Mr. Bennett. It may seem odd that Mr. Bennett should have a chauffeur; but he had—or proposed to have—*pro hac vice*—or *ad hoc;* for this particular job, in fact. Without a car that stuff at Tower Cottage—somewhere at Tower Cottage—would be difficult to shift.

The Sergeant demurred still, by no means for the sake of saving Beaumaroy's skin, but still purely for the reason already given; yet he admitted that he could not name any date on which he could guarantee Beaumaroy's absence from Tower Cottage. "He never leaves the old blighter alone later than eleven o'clock or so, and rarely as late as that."

"Then any night's about the same," said gentleman Bennett; "and now for the scheme, dear N.C.O.!"

Sergeant Hooper despaired of the doors. The house-door might possibly be negotiated, though at the probable cost of arousing the notice of Beaumaroy—and of the old blighter himself. But the door from the parlor into the Tower offered insuperable difficulties. It was always locked; the lock was intricate; he had never so much as seen the key at close quarters and, even had opportunity offered, was quite unpractised in the art of taking impressions of locks—a thing not done with accuracy quite so easily as seems sometimes to be assumed.

"For my own part," said Mr. Bennett with a nod, "I've always inclined to the window. We can negotiate that without any noise to speak of, and it oughtn't to take us more than a few minutes. Just deal boards, I expect! Perhaps the old gentleman and your pal Beaumaroy—the Sergeant spat—will sleep right through it!"

"If they ain't in the Tower itself," suggested the Sergeant gloomily.

"Wherever they may be," said gentleman Bennett, with a touch of irritability—he was himself a sanguine man and disliked a mind fertile in objections—"I suppose the stuff's in the Tower, isn't it?"

"It goes in there, and I've never seen it come out, Mr. Bennett." Here at least a tone of confidence rang in the Sergeant's voice.

"But where in the Tower, Sergeant?"

"'Ow should I know? I've never been in the blooming place."

"It's really rather a queer business," observed Mr. Bennett, allowing himself for a moment, an outside and critical consideration of the matter.

"Damned," said the Sergeant briefly.

"But, once inside, we're bound to find it! Then—with the car—it's in London in forty minutes, and in ten more it's—where it's going to be; where that is needn't worry you, my dear Sergeant."

"What if we're seen from the road?" urged the pessimistic Sergeant.

"There's never a job about which you can't put those questions. What if Ludendorff had known just what Foch was going to do, Sergeant? At any rate anybody who sees us is two miles either way from a police station—and may be a lot farther if he tries to interfere with us! It's a hundred to one against anybody being on the road at that time of night; we'll pray for a dark night and dirty weather—which, so far as I've observed, you generally get in this beastly neighborhood." He leant forward and tapped the Sergeant on the shoulder. "Barring accidents, let's say this day week; meanwhile, Neddy"—he smiled as he interjected. "Neddy is our chauffeur—Neddy and I will make our little plan of attack."

"Don't be too generous! Don't leave all the V.C. chances to me," the Sergeant implored.

"Neddy's fair glutton for 'em! Difficulty is to keep him from murder! And he stands six foot four, and weighs seventeen stone."

"I'll back him up—from be'ind—company in support," grinned the Sergeant, considerably comforted by this description of his coadjutor.

"You'll occupy the station assigned to you, my man," said Mr. Bennett, with an admirable burlesque of the military manner. "The front is wherever a soldier is ordered to be—a fine saying of Lord Kitchener's! Remember it, Sergeant!"

"Yes, sir," said the Sergeant, grinning still.

He found Mr. Bennett on the whole amusing company, though occasionally rather alarming; for instance, there seemed to him to be no particular reason for dragging in Neddy's predilection for murder; though, of course, a man of his inches and weight might commit murder through some trifling and pardonable miscalculation of force. "Same as if that Captain Naylor hit you!" the Sergeant reflected, as he finished the ample portion of rum with which the conversation had been lightened. He felt pleasantly muzzy, and saw Mr. Bennett's cleancut features rather blurred in outline. However, the sandy wig and red mustache which that gentleman wore—in his character as a Boxing Day excursionist—were still salient features even to his eyes. Anybody in the room would have been able to swear to them.

Thus the date of the attack was settled and, if only it had been adhered to, things might have fallen out differently between Doctor Mary and Mr. Beaumaroy. Events would probably have relieved Mary from the necessity of presenting her ultimatum, and she might never have heard that illuminating word "Morocco." But big Neddy the Shover—as his intimate friends were wont to call him—was a man of pleasure as well as of business; he was not a bloke in an office; he liked an ample Christmas vacation and was now taking one with a party of friends at Brighton—all tip-toppers who did the thing in style and spent their money (which was not their money) lavishly. From the attraction of this company—not composed of gentlemen only—Neddy refused to be separated. Mr. Bennett, who was on thorns at the delay, could take it or leave it at that; in any case the job was, in Neddy's opinion (which he expressed with that massive but good-humored scorn which is an appanage of very large men), a leap in the dark, a pig in a poke, blind hookey; for who really knew how much of the stuff the old blighter and his pal had contrived to shift down to the Cottage in the old brown bag. Sometimes it looked light, sometimes it looked heavy; sometimes perhaps it was full of bricks!

In this mood Neddy had to be humored, even though gentlemanly Mr. Bennett sat on thorns. The Sergeant repined less at the delay; he liked the pickings which the job brought him much better than the job itself, standing in wholesome dread of Beaumaroy. It was rather with resignation than with joy that he received from Mr. Bennett the news that Neddy had at last named the day that would suit his High Mightiness—Tuesday the 7th of January it was, and, as it chanced, the very day before Beaumaroy was to start for Morocco! More accurately, the attack would be delivered on the actual day of his departure—if he went. For it was timed for one o'clock in the morning, an hour at which the road across the heath might reasonably be expected to be clear of traffic. This was an especially important point, in view of the fact that the window of the Tower faced towards the road and was but four or five yards distant from it.

After a jovial dinner—rather too jovial in Mr. Bennett's opinion, but that was Neddy's only fault, he would mix pleasure with business—the two set out in an Overland car. Mr. Bennett—whom, by the way, his big friend Neddy called "Mike," and not "Percy," as might have been expected—assumed his sandy wig and red mustache as soon as they were well started; Neddy scorned disguise for the moment, but he had a mask in his pocket. He also had a very nasty little club in the same pocket, whereas Mr. Bennett carried no weapon of offense—merely the tools of his trade, at which he was singularly expert. The friends had worked together before; though Neddy reviled Mike for a coward, and Mike averred with curses, that Neddy would bring them both to the gallows some day, yet they worked well together and had a respect for one another, each allowing for the other's idiosyncrasies. The true spirit of partnership! On it alone can lasting and honorable success be built.

"Just match-boarding, the Sergeant says it is, does he?" asked Neddy, breaking a long silence, which indeed had lasted until they were across Putney Bridge and climbing the Hill.

"Yes, and rotten at that. It oughtn't to take two minutes; then there'll be only the window. Of course we must have a look round first. Then, if the coast's clear, I'll nip in and shove something up against the door of the place while you're following. The Sergeant's to stay on guard at the door of the house, so that we can't be taken in the rear. See?"

"Righto!"

"Then—well, we've got to find the stuff, and when we've found it, you've got to carry it, Neddy. Don't mind if it's a bit heavy, do you?"

"I don't want to overstrain myself," said Neddy jocularly, "but I'll do my best with it, only hope it's there!"

"It must be there. Hasn't got wings, has it? At any rate not till you put it in your pocket, and go out for an evening with the ladies!"

Neddy paid this pleasantry the tribute of a laugh, but he had one more business question to ask:

"Where are we to stow the car? How far off?"

"The Sergeant has picked out a big clump of trees, a hundred yards from the cottage on the Sprotsfield side, and about thirty yards from the road. Pretty clear going to it, bar the bracken—she'll do it easily. There she'll lie, snug as you like. As we go by Sprotsfield, the car won't have to pass the Cottage at all—that's an advantage—and yet it's not over far to carry the stuff."

"Sounds all right," said Neddy placidly, and with a yawn. "Have a drop?"

"No, I won't—and I wish you wouldn't, Neddy. It makes you bad-tempered, and a man doesn't want to be bad-tempered on these jobs."

"Take the wheel a second while I have a drop," said Neddy, just for all the world as if his friend had not spoken. He unscrewed the top of a large flask and took a very considerable "drop." It was only after he had done this with great deliberation that he observed good-naturedly, "And you go to hell, Mike! It's dark, ain't it? That's a bit of all right."

He did not speak again till they were near Sprotsfield. "This Beaumaroy—queer name, ain't it?—he's a big chap, ain't he, Mike?"

"Pretty fair, but, Lord love you, a baby beside yourself."

"Well, now, you told me something the Sergeant said about a man as was (Neddy, unlike his friend, occasionally tripped in his English) really big."

"Oh, that's Naylor—Captain Naylor. But he's not at the cottage; we're not likely to meet him, praise be!"

"Rather wish we were! I want a little bit of exercise," said Neddy.

"Well, I don't know but what Beaumaroy might give you that. The Sergeant's got tales about him at the war."

"Oh, blast these soldiers—they ain't no good." In what he himself regarded as his spare hours, that is to say, the daytime hours wherein the ordinary man labors, Neddy was a highly skilled craftsman, whose only failing was a tendency to be late in the morning and to fall ill about the festive seasons of the year. He made lenses, and, in spite of the failing, his work had been deemed to be of national importance, as indeed it was. But that did not excuse his prejudice against soldiers.

They passed through the outskirts of Sprotsfield; Mike—to use his more familiar name—had made a thorough exploration of the place, and his directions enabled his chauffeur to avoid the central and populous parts of the town. Then they came out on to the open heath, passed Old Place, and presently—about half a mile from Tower Cottage—found Sergeant Hooper waiting for them by the roadside. It was then hard on midnight—a dark cloudy night, very apt for their purpose. With a nod, but without a word, the Sergeant got into the car, and in cautious whispers directed its course to the shelter of the clump of trees; they reached it after a few hundred yards of smooth road and some thirty of bumping over the heath. It afforded a perfect screen from the road, and on the other side there was only untrodden heath, no path or track being visible near it.

Neddy got out of the car, but he did not forget his faithful flask. He offered it to the Sergeant in token of approval. "Good place, Sergeant," he said; "does credit to you, as a beginner. Here, mate, hold on, though. It's evident you ain't accustomed to liquor glasses!"

"When I sits up so late, I gets a kind of a sinking," the Sergeant explained apologetically.

Mike flashed a torch on him for a minute; there was a very uncomfortable look in his little squinty eyes. "Sergeant," he said suavely but gravely, "my friend here relies on you. He's not a safe man to disappoint." He shifted the light suddenly on to Neddy, whose proportions seemed to loom out prodigious from the surrounding darkness. "Are you, Neddy?"

"No, I'm a sensitive chap, I am," said Neddy, smiling. "Don't you go and hurt my pride in you by any sign of weakness, Sergeant."

The Sergeant shivered a little. "I'm game. I'll stick it," he protested valorously.

"You'd better!" Neddy advised.

"All quiet at the Cottage as you came by?" asked Mike.

"Quiet as the grave, for what I see," the Sergeant answered.

"All right. Mike, where are them sandwiches? I feel like a bite. One for the Sergeant too! But no more flask—no, you don't Sergeant! When'll we start, Mike!"

"In about half-an-hour."

"Just nice time for a snack—oysters and stout for you, my darling?" said jovial Neddy. Then—with a change of voice—"Just as well that didn't pass us!"

For the sound of a car came from the road they had just left. It was going in the direction of the Cottage and of Inkston. Captain Alec was taking his betrothed home after a joyful evening of congratulation and welcome.

Chapter 12

The Secret of the Tower

The scene presented by the interior of the Tower, when Beaumaroy softly opened the door and signed to Doctor Mary to step forward and look, was indeed a strange one, a ridiculous yet pathetic mockery of grandeur.

The building was a circular one, rising to a height of some thirty-five feet and having a diameter of about ten. Up to about twelve feet from the floor its walls were draped with red and purple stuffs of coarse material; above them the bare bricks and the rafters of the roof showed naked. In the middle of the floor, with their backs to the door at which Mary and her companion stood, were set two small armchairs of plain and cheap make. Facing them, on a rough dais about three feet high and with two steps leading up to it, stood a large and deep carved oaken armchair. It too was upholstered in purple, and above and around it were a canopy and curtains of the same color. This strange erection was set with its back to the one window—that which Mr. Saffron had caused to be boarded up soon after he entered into occupation. The place was lighted by candles—two tall standards of an ecclesiastical pattern, one on either side of the great chair or throne, and each holding six large candles, all of which were now alight and about half-consumed. On the throne, his spare wasted figure set far back in the recesses of its deep cushioned seat and his feet resting on a high hassock, sat old Mr. Saffron; in his right hand he grasped a scepter, obviously a theatrical "property," but a handsome one, of black wood with gilt ornamentation; his left arm he held close against his side. His eyes were turned up towards the room; his lips were moving as though he were talking, but no sound came.

Such was Doctor Mary's first impression of the scene; but the next moment she took in another feature of it, not less remarkable. To the left of the throne, to her right as she stood in the doorway facing it, there was a fireplace; an empty grate, though the night was cold. Immediately in front of it was, unmistakably, the excavation in the floor which Mr. Penrose had described at the Christmas dinner-party at Old Place—six feet in length by three in breadth, and about four feet deep. Against the wall, close by, stood a sheet of cast iron, which evidently served to cover and conceal the aperture; by it was thrown down, in careless disorder, a strip of the same dull red baize as covered the rest of the floor of the Tower. By the side of the sheet and the piece of carpet there was an old brown leather bag.

Tradition, and Mr. Penrose, had told the truth. Here without doubt was Captain Duggle's grave, the grave he had caused to be dug for himself, but which—be the reason what it might—his body had never occupied. Yet the tomb was not entirely empty. The floor of it was strewn with gold, to what depth Mary could not tell, but it was covered with golden sovereigns; there must be thousands of them. They gleamed under the light of the candles.

Mary turned, startled, inquiring, apprehensive eyes on Beaumaroy. He pressed her arm gently, and whispered:

"I'll tell you presently. Come in. He'll notice us, I expect, in a minute. Mind you curtsey when he sees you!" He led her in, pulling the door to after him, and placed her and himself in front of the two small armchairs opposite Mr. Saffron's throne.

Beaumaroy removed his hand from her arm, but she caught his wrist in one of hers and stood there, holding on to him, breathing quickly, her eyes now set on the figure on the throne.

The old man's lips had ceased to move; his eyes had closed; he lay back in the deep seat, inert, looking half-dead, very pale and waxen in the face. For what seemed a long time he sat thus, motionless and almost without signs of life, while the two stood side by side before him. Mary glanced once at Beaumaroy; his lips were apart in that half humorous, half compassionate smile; there was no hint of impatience in his bearing.

At last Mr. Saffron opened his eyes, and saw them; there was intelligence in his look, though his body did not move. Mary was conscious of a low bow from Beaumaroy; she remembered the caution he had given her, and herself made a deep curtsey; the old man made a slight inclination of his handsome white head. Then, after another long pause, a movement passed over his body—excepting his left arm. She saw that he was trying to rise from his seat, but that he had barely the strength to achieve his purpose. But he persisted in his effort, and in the end rose slowly and tremulously to his feet.

Then, utterly without warning, in a sudden and shocking burst of that high, voluble, metallic speech which Captain Alec had heard through the ceiling of the parlor, he began to address them, if indeed it were they whom he addressed, and not some phantom audience of Princes, Marshals, Admirals, or trembling sheep-like re emits. It was difficult to hear the words, hopeless to make out the sense. It was a farrago of nonsense, part of his own inventing, part (as it seemed) wild and confused reminiscences of the published speeches of the man he aped, all strung together on some invisible thread of insane reasoning, delivered with a mad vehemence and intensity that shook and seemed to rend his feeble frame.

"We must stop him, we must stop him," Mary suddenly whispered. "He'll kill himself if he goes on like this!"

"I've never been able to stop him," Beaumaroy whispered back. "Hush! If he hears us speaking he'll be furious, and carry on worse."

The old man's blue eyes fixed themselves on Beaumaroy—of Mary he took no heed. He pointed at Beaumaroy with his scepter, and from him to the gleaming gold in Captain Duggle's grave. A streak of coherency, a strand of mad logic, now ran through his hurtling words; the money was there, Beaumaroy was to take it—to-day, to-day!—to take it to Morocco, to raise the tribes, to set Africa aflame. He was to scatter it—broadcast, broadcast! There was no end to it—don't spare it! "There's millions, millions of it!" he shouted, and achieved a weird wild majesty in a final cry, "God with us!"

Then he fell—tumbled back in utter collapse into the recesses of the great chair. His scepter fell from his nerveless hand and rolled down the steps of the dais; the impetus it gathered carried it, rolling still, across the floor to the edge of the open pit; for an instant it lay poised on the edge, and then fell with a jangle of sound on the carpet of golden coins that lined Captain Duggle's grave.

"Quick! Get my bag—I left it in the passage," whispered Mary, as she started forward, up the dais, to the old man's side. "And brandy, if you've got it," she called after Beaumaroy, as he turned to the door to do her bidding.

Beaumaroy was gone no more than a minute. When he came back, with the bag hitched under his arm, a decanter of brandy in one band and a glass in the other, Mary was leaning over the throne, with her arm round the old man. His eyes were open, but he was inert and motionless. Beaumaroy poured out some brandy, and gave it into Mary's free hand. But when Mr. Saffron saw Beaumaroy by his side, he gave a sudden twist of his body, wrenched himself away from Mary's arm, and flung himself on his trusted friend. "Hector, I'm in danger! They're after me! They'll shut me up!"

Beaumaroy put his strong arms about the frail old body. "Oh no, sir, oh, no!" he said in low, comforting, half-bantering tones. "That's the old foolishness, sir, if I may so say. You're perfectly safe with me. You ought to trust me by now, sir, really you ought."

"You swear, you swear it's all right, Hector?"

"Right as rain, sir," Beaumaroy assured him cheerfully.

Very feebly the old man moved his right hand towards the open grave. "Plenty—plenty! All yours, Hector! For—for the Cause—God's with us!" His head fell forward on Beaumaroy's breast; for an instant again he raised it, and looked in the face of his friend. A smile came on his lips. "I know I can trust you. I'm safe with you, Hector." His head fell forward again; his whole body was relaxed; he gave a sigh of peace. Beaumaroy lifted him in his arms

125

and very gently set him back in his great chair, placing his feet again on the high footstool.

"I think it's all over," he said, and Mary saw tears in his eyes.

Then Mary herself collapsed; she sank down on the dais and broke into weeping. It had all been so pitiful, and somehow so terrible. Her quick tumultuous sobbing sounded through the place which the vibrations of the old man's voice had lately filled.

She felt Beaumaroy's hand on her shoulder. "You must make sure," he said, in a low voice. "You must make your examination."

With trembling hands she did it—she forced herself to it, Beaumaroy aiding her. There was no doubt. Life had left the body which reason had left long before. His weakened heart had not endured the last strain of mad excitement. The old man was dead.

Her face showed Beaumaroy the result of her examination, if he had ever doubted of it. She looked at him, then made a motion of her hand towards the body. "We must—we must—" she stammered, the tears still rolling down her cheeks.

"Presently," he said. "There's plenty of time. You're not fit to do that now—and no more am I, to tell the truth. We'll rest for half an hour, and then get him upstairs, and—and do the rest. Come with me!" He put his hand lightly within her arm. "He will rest quietly on his throne for a little while. He's not afraid any more. He's at rest."

Still with his arm in Mary's, he bent forward and kissed the old man on the forehead. "I shall miss you, old friend," he said. Then, with gentle insistence, he led Mary away. They left the old man, propped up by the high stool on

126

which his feet rested, seated far back in the great chair, hard by Captain Duggle's grave, where the scepter lay on a carpet of gold. The tall candles burnt on either side of his throne, imparting a far-off semblance of ceremonial state.

Thus died, unmarried, in the seventy-first year of his age, Aloysius William Saffron, formerly of Exeter, Surveyor and Auctioneer. He had run, on the whole, a creditable course; starting from small beginnings, and belonging to a family more remarkable for eccentricity than for any solid merit, he had built up a good practice; he had made money and put it by; he enjoyed a good name for financial probity. But he was held to be a vain, fussy, self-important, peacocky fellow; very self-centered also and (as Beaumaroy had indicated) impatient of the family and social obligations which most men recognize, even though often unwillingly. As the years gathered upon his head, these characteristics were intensified. On the occasion of some trifling set-back in business—a rival cut him out in a certain negotiation—He threw up everything and disappeared from his native town. Thenceforward nothing was heard of him there, save that he wrote occasionally to his cousin, Sophia Radbolt, and her husband, both of whom he most cordially hated, whose claims to his notice, regard, or assistance he had, of late years at least, hotly resented. Yet he wrote to them—wrote them vaunting and magniloquent letters, hinting darkly of great doings and great riches. In spite of their opinion of him, the Radbolts came to believe perhaps half of what he said; he was old and without other ties; their thirst for his money was greedy. Undoubtedly the Radbolts would dearly have loved to get hold of him and—somehow—hold him fast.

When he came to Tower Cottage—it was in the first year of the war—he was precariously sane; it was only gradually that his fundamental and constitutional vices and foibles turned to a morbid growth. First came intensified hatred and suspicion of the Radbolts—they were after him and his money! Then, through hidden processes of mental distortion, there grew the conviction that he was of high importance, a great man, the object of great conspiracies, in which the odious Radbolts were but instruments. It was, no doubt, the course of public events, culminating in the Great War, which gave to his mania its special turn, to his delusion its monstrous (but, as Doctor Mary was aware, by no means unprecedented) character. By the time of his meeting with Beaumaroy the delusion was complete; through all the second half of 1918 he followed—so far as his mind could now follow anything rationally—in his own person and fortunes the fate of the man whom he believed himself to be, appropriating the hopes, the fears, the imagined ambitions, the physical infirmity, of that self-created other self.

But he wrapped it all in deep secrecy, for, as the conviction of his true identity grew complete, his fears were multiplied. Radbolts indeed! The whole of Christendom—Principalities and Powers—were on his track. They would shut him up, kill him perhaps! Cunningly he hid his secret—save what could not be entirely hidden, the physical deformity. But he hid it with his shawl; he never ate out of his own house; the combination knife-and-fork was kept sedulously hidden. Only to Beaumaroy did he reveal the hidden thing; and, later, on Beaumaroy's persuasion, he let into the portentous secret one faithful servant—Beaumaroy's unsavory retainer, Sergeant Hooper.

He never accepted Hooper as more than a distasteful necessity—somebody must wait on him and do him menial service; he was not feared, indeed, for surely such a dog would not dare to be false, but cordially disliked. Beaumaroy won him from the beginning. Whom he conceived him to be Beaumaroy himself never knew, but he opened his heart to him unreservedly. Of him he had no suspicion; to him he looked for safety and for the realization of his cherished dreams. Beaumaroy soothed his terrors and humored him in all things—what was the good of doing anything else, asked Beaumaroy's philosophy. He loved Beaumaroy far more than he had loved anybody except himself in all his life. At the end, through the wild tangle of mad imaginings, there ran this golden thread of human affection; it gave the old man hours of peace, sometimes almost of sanity.

So he came to his death, directly indeed of a long-standing organic disease, yet veritably self-destroyed. And so he sat now, dead amidst his shabby parody of splendor. He had done with thrones; he had even done with Tower Cottage—unless indeed his pale shade were to hold nocturnal converse with the robust and flamboyant ghost of Captain Duggle; the one vaunting his unreal vanished greatness, mouthing orations and mimicking pomp; the other telling, in language garnished with strange and horrible oaths, of those dark and lurid terrors which once had driven him from this very place, leaving it ablaze behind. A strange couple they would make, and strange would be their conversation!

Yet the tenement which had housed the old man's deranged spirit, empty as now it was—aye, emptier than Duggle's tomb—was still to be witness of one more earthly scene and unwittingly bear part in it.

Chapter 13

Right of Conquest

What has been related of Mr. Saffron's life before he ascended the throne on which he still sat in the Tower represented all that Beaumaroy knew of his old friend before they met—indeed he knew scarcely as much. He told the brief story to Doctor Mary in the parlor. She heard him listlessly; all that was not much to the point on which her thoughts were set, and did not answer the riddle which the scene in the Tower put to her. She was calm now—and ashamed that she had ever lost her calmness.

"Well, there was the situation as I understood it when I took on the job—or quite soon afterwards. He thought that he was being pursued; in a sense he was. If these Radbolts found out the truth, they certainly would pursue him, try to shut him up, and prevent him from making away with his money or leaving it to anybody else. I didn't at all know at first what a tidy lot he had. He hated the Radbolts; even after he ceased to know them as cousins, he remained very conscious of them always; they were enemies, spies, secret service people on his track—poor old boy! Well, why should they have him and his money? I didn't see it. I don't see it to this day."

Mary was in Mr. Saffron's armchair. Beaumaroy stood before the fire. She looked up at him.

"They seem to have more right than anybody else. And you know—you knew—that he was mad."

"His being mad gives them no right! Oh, well, it's no use arguing. In the end I suppose they had rights—of a kind; a right by law, I suppose—though I never knew the law and don't want to—to shut the old man up, and make him damned miserable, and get the money for themselves. That sounds just the sort of right the law does give people over other people—because Aunt Betsy married Uncle John fifty years ago, and was probably infernally sorry for it!"

Mary smiled. "A matter of principle with you, was it, Mr. Beaumaroy?"

"No—instinct, I think. It's my instinct to be against the proper thing, the regular thing, the thing that deals hardly with an individual in the name of some highly nebulous general principle."

"Like discipline?" she put in, with a reminiscence of Major-General Punnit.

He nodded. "Yes, that's one case of it. And then, the situation amused me. I think that had more to do with it than anything else at first. It amused me to play up to his delusions. I suggested the shawl as useful on our walks—and thereby got him to take wholesome exercise; that ought to appeal to you, Doctor! I got him the combination knife-and-fork; that made him enjoy his meals— also good for him, Doctor! But I didn't do these things because they were good for him, but because they amused me. They never amused Hooper, he's a dull, surly, and— I'm inclined to believe—treacherous dog."

"Who is he?"

"Sacked from the Army—sent to quod. Just a jail-bird whom I've kept loose. But the things did amuse me, and it was that at first. But then—" he paused.

Looking at him again, Mary saw a whimsical tenderness expressed in his eyes and smile. "The poor chap was so overwhelmingly grateful. He thought me the one indubitably faithful adherent that he had. And so I was too—though not in the way he thought. And he trusted me absolutely. Well, was I to give him up—to the law, and the Radbolts, and the jailers of an asylum—a man who trusted me like that?"

"But he was mad," objected Doctor Mary obstinately.

"A man has his feelings, or may have, even when he's mad. He trusted me and he loved me, Doctor Mary. Won't you allow that I've my case—so far?" She made no sign of assent. "Well then, I loved him—does that go any better with you? If it doesn't, I'm in a bad way; be cause what I'm giving you now is the strong part of my case."

"I don't see why you should put what you call your case to me at all, Mr. Beaumaroy."

He looked at her in a reproachful astonishment. "But you seemed touched by—by what we saw in the Tower. I thought the old man's death and faith had appealed to you. It seems to me that people can't go through a thing like that together without feeling—well, some sort of comradeship. But if you've no sort of feeling of that kind—well, I don't want to put my case."

"Go on with your case," said Doctor Mary, after a moment's silence.

"Though it isn't really that I want to put a case for myself at all. But I don't mind owning that I'd like you to understand about it—before I clear out."

She looked at him questioningly, but put no spoken question. Beaumaroy sat down on the stool opposite to her, and poked the fire.

"I can't get away from it, can I? There was something else you saw in the Tower, wasn't there, and I dare say that you connect it with a conversation that we had together a little while ago? Well, I'll tell you about that. Oh, well, of course I must, mustn't I?"

"I should like to hear." Her bitterness was gone; he had come now to the riddle.

"He was a King to himself," Beaumaroy resumed thoughtfully, "but in fact I was king over him. I could do anything I liked with him. I had him. I possessed him—by right of conquest. The right of conquest seemed a big thing to me; it was about the only sort of right that I'd seen anything of for three years and more. Yes, it was—and is—a big thing, a real thing—the one right in the whole world that there's no doubt about. Other rights are theories, views, preachments! Right of conquest is a fact. I had it. I could make him do what I liked, say what I liked, sign what I liked. Do you begin to see where I found myself? I say found myself, because really it was a surprise to me. At first I thought he was in a pretty small way—he only gave me a hundred a year besides my keep. True, he always talked of his money, but I set that down mainly to his delusion. But it was true that he had a lot—really a lot. A good bit besides what you saw in there; he must have speculated cleverly, I think, he couldn't have made it all in his business. Doctor Mary, how much gold do you think there is in the grave in there?"

"I haven't the least idea. Thousands? Where did you get it?"

"Oh yes, thousands—and thousands. We got it mostly from the aliens in the East End; they'd hoarded it, you know; but they were willing to sell at a premium. The premium rose up to last month; then it dropped a little—not much, though, because we'd exhausted some of the most obvious sources. I carried every sovereign of that money in the grave down from London in my brown bag." He smiled reflectively. "Do you know how much a thousand sovereigns weigh, Doctor Mary?"

"I haven't the least idea," said Mary again. She was leaning forward now, listening intently, and watching Beaumaroy's face with absorbed interest.

"Seventeen and three-quarter pounds avoirdupois—that's the correct weight. The first time or two we didn't get much—they were still shy of us. But after that we made some heavy; hauls. Twice we brought down close on two thousand. Once there was three thousand, almost to a sovereign. Even men trained to the work—bullion porters, as they call them at the Bank of England—reckon five bags of a thousand, canvas bags not much short of a foot long and six inches across, you know—they reckon five of them a full load—and wouldn't care to go far with them either. The equivalent of three of them was quite enough for me to carry from Inkston station up to the Cottage—trying to look as if I were carrying nothing of any account! One hasn't got to pretend to be carrying nothing in full marching kit—nor to carry it all in one hand. And he'd never trust himself in a cab—might be kidnapped, you see! I don't know exactly, but from what he said I reckon we've brought down, on our Wednesday trips, about two-thirds of all he had. Now you've probably gathered what his idea was. He knew he was disguised as Saffron—and very proud of the way he lived up to the character. As Saffron, he realized the money by driblets—turned his securities into notes, his notes into gold. But he'd lost all knowledge that the money was his own—made by himself—himself Saffron. He thought it was saved out of the wreck of his Imperial fortune. It was to be dedicated to restoring the Imperial cause. He himself could not attempt, at present, to get out of England, least of all carrying pots of gold coin. But he believed that I could. I was to go to Morocco and so on, and raise the country for him, taking as much as I could, and coming back for more! He had no doubt at all of my coming back! In fact it wouldn't have been much easier for me to get out of the country with the money than it would have been for the authentic Kaiser himself. But, Doctor Mary, what would have been possible was for me to go somewhere else, or even back to the places we knew of, for no questions were asked there—put that money back into notes, or securities in my own name, and tell him I had carried out the Morocco programme. He had no sense of time, he would have suspected nothing."

"That would have been mere and sheer robbery," said Mary.

"Oh yes, it would," Beaumaroy agreed. "And, if I'd done it, and deserted him, I should have deserved to be hanged. That was hardly my question. As long as he lived, I meant to stick by him; but he was turned seventy, frail, with heart-disease, and, as I understand, quite likely to sink into general paralysis. Well, if I was to exercise my right of conquest and get the fruits of conquest, two ways seemed open. There could be a will; you'll remember my consulting you on that point and your reply?"

"Did he make a will?" asked Mary quickly.

"No. A will was open to serious objections. Even supposing your evidence—which, of course, I wanted in case of need—had been satisfactory, a fight with the Radbolts would have been unpleasant. Worse than that—as long as I lived I should have been blackmailed by Sergeant Hooper, who knew Mr. Saffron's condition, though he didn't know about the money here. Even before you found out about my poor old friend, I had decided against a will—though, perhaps, I might have squared the Radbolts by just taking this little place—and its contents—and letting them take the rest. That too became impossible after your discovery. There remained then, the money in the Tower. I could make quite sure of that, wait for his death, and then enjoy it. And, upon my word, why shouldn't I? He'd have been much gratified by my going to Morocco; and he'd certainly much sooner that I had the money—if it couldn't go to Morocco—than that the Radbolts should get it. That was the way the question presented itself to me; and I'm a poor man, with no obvious career before me. The right of conquest appealed to me strongly, Doctor Mary."

"I can see that you may have been greatly tempted," said Mary in a grave and troubled voice. "And the circumstances did enable you to make excuses for what you thought of doing."

"Excuses? You won't even go so far as to call it a doubtful case? One that a casuist could argue either way?" Beaumaroy was smiling again now.

"Even if I did, men of—"

"Yes, Doctor Mary—of sensitive honor!"

"Decide doubtful cases against themselves in money matters."

"Oh, I say, is that doctrine current in business circles? I've been in business myself, and I doubt it."

"They do—men of real honor," Mary persisted.

"So that's how great fortunes are made? That's how individuals—to say nothing of nations—rise to wealth and power! And I never knew it," Beaumaroy reflected in a gentle voice. His eye caught Mary's, and she gave a little laugh. "By deciding doubtful cases against themselves! Dear me, yes!"

"I didn't say they rose to greatness and power."

"Then the people who do rise to greatness and power—and the nations—don't they go by right of conquest, Doctor Mary? Don't they decide cases in their own favor?"

"Did you really mean to—to take the money?"

"I'll tell you as near as I can. I meant to do my best for my old man. I meant him to live as long as he could, and to live free, unpersecuted, as happy as he could be made. I meant that, because I loved him, and he loved me. Well, I've lost him; I'm alone in the world." The last words were no appeal to Mary; for the moment he seemed to have forgotten her; he was speaking out of his own heart to himself. Yet the words thereby touched her to a livelier pity; you are very lonely when there is nobody to whom you have affection's right to complain of loneliness.

"But after that, if I saw him to his end in peace, if I brought that off, well, then I rather think that I should have stuck to the money. Yes, I rather think so."

"You've managed to mix things up so!" Mary complained. "Your devotion to Mr. Saffron—for that I could forgive you keeping his secret, and fooling me, and all of us. But then you mix that up with the money!"

"It was mixed up with it. I didn't do the mixing."

"What are you going to do now?" she asked with a sudden curiosity.

"Oh, now? Now the thing's all different. You've seen, you know, and even I can't offer you a partnership in the cash, can I? If I weren't an infernally poor conspirator, I should have covered up the Captain's grave, and made everything neat and tidy before I came to fetch you, because I knew he might go back to the Tower. On his bad nights he always made me open the grave, and spread out the money, make a show of it, you know. Then it had to be put back in bags—the money bags lived in the brown leather bag—and the grave had to be fastened down. Altogether it was a good bit of work. I'd just got it open, and the money spread out, when he turned bad—a sort of collapse like the one you saw; and I was so busy getting him to bed that I forgot the cursed grave and the money— just as I forgot to put away the knife-and-fork before you called the first time, and you saw through me!"

"If you're not a good conspirator, it's another reason for not conspiring, Mr. Beaumaroy. I know you conspired for him first of all, but—"

"Well, he's safe, he's at peace. It can all come out now, and it must. You know, and you must tell the truth. I don't know whether they can put me in prison. I should hardly think they'd bother, if they get the money all right. In any case I don't care much. Lord, what a lot of people'll say 'I told you so—bad egg, that Beaumaroy!' No, I don't care. My old man's safe; I've won my big game after all, Doctor Mary!"

"I don't believe you cared about the money really!" she cried. "That really was a game to you, I think, a trick you liked to play on us respectables!"

139

He smiled at her confidentially. "I do like beating the respectables," he admitted. Then he looked at his watch. "I must do what has to be done for the old man. But it's late—hard on one o'clock. You must be tired—and it's a sad job."

"No, I'll help you. I—I've been in hospitals, you know. Only do go first, and cover up that horrible place, and hide that wretched money before I go into the Tower. Will you?" She gave a shiver, as her imagination renewed the scene which the Tower held.

"You needn't come into the Tower at all. He's as light as a feather—I've lifted him into bed often. I can lift him now. If you really wish to help, will you go up to his room, and get things ready?" As he spoke, he crossed to the sideboard, took up a bedroom candlestick, and lighted it from one that stood on the table. "And you'll see about the body being taken to the mortuary, won't you? I shall communicate with the Radbolts—fully; they'll take charge of the funeral, I suppose. Well, he won't know anything about that now, thank God!" There was the slightest tremor in his voice as he spoke.

Mary did not take the candle. "I've said some hard things to you, Mr. Beaumaroy. I dare say I've sounded very self-righteous." He raised his hand in protest, but she went on: "So I should like to say one different thing to you, since we're to part after to-night. You've shown yourself a good friend, good and true as a man could have."

"I loved my old man," said Beaumaroy.

It was his only plea. To Mary it seemed a good one. He had loved his poor old madman; and he had served him faithfully. "Yes, the old man found a good friend in you; I hope you will find good friends too. Oh, I do hope it! Because that's what you want."

"I should be very glad if I could think that, in spite of everything, I had found one here in this place—even although she can be a friend only in memory."

Mary paused for a moment, then gave him her hand. "I know you much better after tonight. My memory of you will be a kind one. Now to our work!"

"Yes—and thank you. I thank you more deeply than you imagine."

He gave her the candle and followed her to the passage.

"You know where the room is. I shall put the—the place—straight, and then bring him up. I sha'n't be many minutes—ten, perhaps. The cover's rather hard to fit."

Mary nodded from the top of the stairs. Strained by the events of the night, and by the talk to Beaumaroy, she was again near tears; her eyes were bright in the light of the candle, and told of nervous excitement. Beaumaroy went back into the parlor, on his way to the Tower. Suddenly he stopped and stood dead still, listening intently.

Mary busied herself upstairs, making her preparations with practiced skill and readiness. Her agitation did not interfere with her work—there her training told—but of her inner mind it had full possession. She was afraid to be alone—there in that cottage. She longed for another clasp of that friendly hand. Well, he would come soon; but he must bring his burden with him. When she had finished what she had to do, she sat down, and waited.

Beaumaroy waited too, outside the door leading to the Tower.

Chapter 14

The Scepter in the Grave

Sergeant Hooper took up his appointed position on the flagged path that led up to the cottage door. His primary task was to give warning if anybody should come out of the door; a secondary one was to give the alarm in case of interruption by passers-by on the road—an unlikely peril this latter, in view of the hour, the darkness of the night, and the practiced noiselessness with which Mike might be relied upon to do his work. Here then the Sergeant was left, after being accorded another nip from the flask—which, however, Neddy kept in his own hands this time—and a whispered but vigorously worded exhortation to keep up his courage.

Neddy, the Shover, and gentlemanly Mike tiptoed off to the window, on the right hand side of the door as one approached the house from the road. The bottom of the window was about seven feet from the ground. Neddy bent down and offered his broad back as a platform to his companion. Mike mounted thereon and began his work. That, in itself, was child's play to him; the matchboarding was but lightly nailed on; the fastenings came away in a moment under the skillful application of his instrument; the window sash behind was not even bolted, for the bolt had perished with time and had not been replaced. So far, very good! But at this early point Mike received his first surprise. He could not see much of the interior; a tall curtain stretched across the entire breadth of the window, distant about two feet from it; but he could see that the room was lighted up.

Very cautiously he completed his work on the match-boarding, handing down each plank to Neddy when he had detached it. Then he cut out a pane of glass—it was all A.B.C. to him—put his hand in and raised the sash a little; then it was simple to push it up from below. But the sash had not been raised for years; it stuck; when it yielded to his efforts, it gave a loud creak. He flung one leg over the window-sill and sat poised there, listening. The room was lighted up; but if there were anyone in it, he must be asleep, or very hard of hearing, or that creak would have aroused his attention.

Released from his office as a support, Neddy rose, and hauled himself up by his arms till he could see in the window. "Lights!" he whispered. Mike nodded and got in—on the dais, behind the curtain. Neddy scrambled up after him, finding some help from a stunted but sturdy old apple tree that grew against the wall. Now they were both inside, behind the tall curtain.

"Come on," Mike whispered. "We must see if there's anybody here, and, if there isn't, put out the light." For on either side of the curtain there was room for a streak of light which might by chance be seen from the road.

Mike advanced round the left-side edge of the curtain; he had perceived by now that it formed the back of some structure, though he could not yet see of what nature the structure was; nor was he now examining. For as he stepped out on the dais at the side of the canopy, his eyes were engrossed by another feature of this strange apartment. He stretched back his hand and caught hold of Neddy's brawny arm, pulling him forward. "See that— that hole, Neddy?"

For the moment they forgot the lights; they forgot the possibility of an occupant of the room—which indeed was, save for their own whispers, absolutely still; they stood looking at the strange hole, and then into one another's faces, for a few seconds. Then they stole softly nearer to it. "That's a blasted funny 'ole!" breathed Neddy. "Look's like a bloke's—"

Mike's fingers squeezed his arm tighter, evidently again claiming his attention. "My hat, we needn't look far for the stuff!" he whispered. An uneasy whisper it was; the whole place looked queer, and that hole was uncanny—it had its contents.

Yet they approached nearer; they came to the edge and stood looking in. As though he could not believe the mere sight of his eyes, big Neddy crouched down, reached out his hand, and took up Mr. Saffron's scepter. With a look of half-scared amazement he held it up for his companion's inspection. Mike eyed it uneasily, but his thoughts were getting back to business. He stole softly off to the door, with intent to see whether it was locked; he stooped down to examine it and perceived that it was not. It would be well, then, to barricade it, and he turned round to look for some heavy bit of furniture suitable for his purpose, something that would delay the entrance of an intruder and give them notice of the interruption.

As he turned, his body suddenly stiffened; only his trained instinct prevented him from crying out. There was an occupant of the room—there, in the great chair between the tall candlesticks on the dais. An old man sat—half lay—there; asleep, it seemed; his eyes were shut. The color of his face struck Gentleman Mike as being peculiar. But everything in that place was peculiar; like a great tomb—a blooming mausoleum—the whole place was. Though he had the reputation of being an *esprit fort,* Mike felt uncomfortable. Cold and clammy too, the beastly place was!

Still—business is business. Letting the matter of the unlocked door wait for the moment, he began to steal cat-like across the floor towards the dais. He had to investigate; also he really ought to put out those candles; it was utterly unprofessional to leave them alight. But he could not conquer a feeling that the place would seem still more peculiar when they were put out.

Big Neddy's eyes had not followed his comrade to the door; they had been held by the queer hole and its queer contents—by the gleaming gold that strewed its floor, by the mock symbol of majesty which he had lifted from it and still held in his hand, by the oddly suggestive shape and dimensions of the hole itself. But now he raised his eyes from these things and looked across at Mike, mutely asking what he thought of matters. He saw Mike stealing across the floor, looking very, very hard at—something.

Mute as Neddy's inquiry was, Mike seemed somehow aware of it. He raised his hand, as though to enjoin silence, and then pointed it in front of him, raised to the level of his head. Neddy turned round to look in the direction indicated. He saw the throne and its silent occupant—the waxen-faced old man who sat there, seeming to preside over the scene, whose head was turned towards him, whose closed eyes would open directly on his face if their lids were lifted.

Neddy feared no living man; so he was accustomed to boast, and with good warrant. But was that man living? How came he up there? And what had he to do with the queer-shaped hole that had all that gold in it? And the thing he held in his own hand? Did that belong to the old man up there? Had he flung it into the hole? Or (odd fancies began to assail big Neddy) had he left it behind him when he got out? And would he, by chance, come down to look for it?

Mike's hand, stretched out from his body towards his friend, now again enjoined silence. He was at the foot of the dais; he was going up its steps. He was no good in a scrap, but he had a nerve in some things! He was up the steps now, and leaning forward; he was looking hard in the old man's face; his own was close to it. He laid hold of one of the old man's arms, it happened to be that left arm of Mr. Saffron's, lifted it, and let it fall again; it fell back just in the position from which he had lifted it. Then he straightened himself up, looking a trifle green perhaps, but reassured, and called out to Mike, in a penetrating whisper, "He's a stiff un all right!"

Yes! But then, what of the grave? Because it was a grave and nothing else; there was no getting away from it. What of the grave, and what about the scepter?

And what was Mike going to do now? He was tiptoeing to the edge of the dais. He was moving towards one of the high candlesticks, the top of which was a little below the level of his head, as he stood raised on the dais beside the throne. He leant forward towards the candles; his intent was obvious.

But big Neddy was not minded that he should carry it out, could not suffer him to do it. With the light of the candles—well, at all events you could see what was happening; you could see where you were, and where anybody else was. But in the dark—left to torches which illuminated only bits of the place, and which perhaps you mightn't switch on in time or turn in the right direction; if you were left like that, anybody might be anywhere, and on to you before you knew it!

"Let them lights alone, Mike!" he whispered hoarsely. "I'll smash your 'ead in if you put them lights out!"

Mike had conquered his own fit of nerves, not without some exercise of will, and had not given any notice to his companion's, which was considerably more acute; perhaps the constant use of that roomy flask had contributed to that, though lack of a liberal education (such as Mike had enjoyed and misused) must also bear its share of responsibility. He was amazed at this violent and threatening interruption. He gave a funny little skip backwards on the dais; his heel came thereby in contact with the high hassock on which Mr. Saffron's feet rested. The hassock was shifted; one foot fell from it on to the dais, and Mr. Saffron's body fell a little forward from out of the deep recess of his great chair. To big Neddy's perturbed imagination it looked as if Mr. Saffron had set one foot upon the floor of the dais and was going to rise from his seat, perhaps to come down from the dais, to come nearer to his grave—to ask for his scepter.

It was too much for Neddy. He shuddered, he could not help it; and the scepter dropped from his hand. It fell from his hand back into the grave again; under its impact the gold coins in the grave again jangled.

Beaumaroy had, by this time, been standing close outside the door for about two minutes; he had lighted a cigarette from the candle on the parlor table. The sounds that he thought he heard were not conclusive; creaks and cracks did sometimes come from the boarded-up window and the rafters of the roof. But the sound of the jangling gold was conclusive; it must be due in some way to human agency; and in the circumstances human agency must mean a thief.

Beaumaroy's mind leapt to the Sergeant. Ten to one it was the Sergeant! He had long been after the secret; he had at last sniffed it out, and was helping himself! It seemed to Beaumaroy a disgusting thing to do, with the dead man sitting there. But that was sentiment. Sentiment was not to be expected of the Sergeant, and disgusting things were.

Then he suddenly recalled Alec Naylor's story of the two men, one tall and slight, one short and stumpy, who had reconnoitered Tower Cottage. The Sergeant had an accomplice, no doubt. He listened again. He heard the scrape of metal on metal, as when a man gathers up coins in his hand out of a heap. Yet he stood where he was, smoking still. Thoughts were passing rapidly through his brain, and they brought a smile to his lips.

Let them take it! Why not? It was no care to him now! Doctor Mary had to tell the truth about it, and so, consequently, had he himself. It belonged to the Radbolts. Oh, damn the Radbolts! He would have risked his life for it if the old man had lived, but he wasn't going to risk his life for the Radbolts. Let the rascals get off with the stuff, or as much as they could carry! He was all right. Doctor Mary could testify that he hadn't taken it. Let them carry off the infernal stuff! Incidentally he would be well rid of the Sergeant, and free from any of his importunities, from whines and threats alike; it was not an unimportant, if a minor, consideration.

Yet it was a disgusting thing to do—it certainly was; and the Sergeant would think that he had scored a triumph. Over his benefactor too, his protector, Beaumaroy reflected with a satiric smile. The Sergeant certainly deserved a fright—and, if possible, a licking. These administered, he could be kicked out; perhaps—oh, yes, poor brute!—with a handful of the Radbolts' money. They would never miss it, as they did not know how much there was, and such a diversion of their legal property in no way troubled Beaumaroy's conscience.

And the accomplice? He shrugged his shoulders. The Sergeant was, as he well knew from his military experience of that worthy man, an arrant coward. He would show no fight. If the accomplice did, Beaumaroy was quite in the mood to oblige him. But while he tackled one fellow, the other might get off with the money—with as much as he could carry. For all that it was merely Radbolt money now; in the end Beaumaroy could not stomach the idea of that—the idea that either of the dirty rogues in there should get off with the money. And it was foolish to attack them on the front on which they expected to be attacked. Quickly his mind formed another plan. He turned, stole softly out of the parlor, and along the passage towards the front door of the cottage.

After Neddy had dropped Mr. Saffron's scepter into Captain Duggle's grave (had he known that it was Captain Duggle's, and not been a prey to the ridiculous but haunting fancy that it had been destined for, or even—oh, these errant fancies—already occupied by, Mr. Saffron himself, Neddy would have been less agitated) Mike dealt with him roundly. In bitter hissing whispers, and in language suited thereto, he pointed out the folly of vain superstitions, of childish fears and sick imaginings which interfered with business and threatened its success. His eloquent reasoning, combined with a lively desire to get out of the place as soon as possible, so far wrought on Neddy that he produced the sack which he had brought with him, and held its mouth open, though with trembling hands, while Mike scraped up handful after handful of gold coins and poured them into it. They were busily engaged on their joint task as Beaumaroy stole along the passage and, reaching the front door, again stood listening.

The Sergeant was still keeping his vigil before the door. He had no doubt that it was locked; did not Beaumaroy see Mrs. Wiles and himself out of it every evening—the back door to the little house led only on to the heath behind and gave no direct access to the road—and lock it after them with a squeaking key? He would have warning enough if anyone turned the key now. He was looking towards the road; a surprise was more possible from that quarter; his back was towards the door and only a very little way from it.

But when Beaumaroy had entered with Doctor Mary, he had not re-locked the door; he opened it now very gently and cautiously, and saw the Sergeant's back—there was no mistaking it. Without letting his surprise—for he had confidently supposed the Sergeant to be in the Tower—interfere with the instant action called for by the circumstances, he flung out his long right arm, caught the Sergeant round the neck with a throttling grip, and dragged him backwards into the house. The man was incapable of crying out; no sound escaped from him which could reach the Tower. Beaumaroy set him softly on the floor of the passage. "If you stir or speak, I'll strangle you!" he whispered. There was enough light from the passage lamp to enable the Sergeant to judge, by the expression of his face, that he spoke sincerely. The Sergeant did not dare even to rub his throat, though it was feeling very sore and uncomfortable.

There was a row of pegs on the passage wall, just inside the door. On them, among hats, caps, and coats—and also Mr. Saffron's gray shawl—hung two long neck-scarves, comforters that the keen heath winds made very acceptable on a walk. Beaumaroy took them, and tied his prisoner hand and foot. He had just completed this operation, in the workmanlike fashion which he had learnt on service, when he heard a footstep on the stairs. Looking up, he saw Doctor Mary standing there.

Her waiting in the room above had seemed long to her. Her ears had been expecting the sound of Beaumaroy's tread as he mounted the stairs, laden with his burden. That sound had not come; instead, there had been the soft, just audible, plop of the Sergeant's body as it dropped on the floor of the passage. It occurred to her that Beaumaroy had perhaps had some mishap with his burden, or found difficulty with it. She was coming downstairs to offer her help. Seeing what she saw now, she stood still in surprise.

Beaumaroy looked up at her and smiled. "No cause for alarm," he said, "but I've got to go out for a minute. Keep an eye on this rascal, will you? Oh, and, Doctor Mary, if he tries to move or untie himself, just take the parlor poker and hit him over the head! Thanks. You don't mind, de you? And you, Sergeant, remember what I said!"

152

With these words Beaumaroy slipped out of the door, and softly closed it behind him.

Chapter 15

A Normal Case

When Captain Alec brought his *fiancée* home after the dinner of welcome and congratulation at Old Place, it was nearly twelve o'clock. Jeanne, however—in these days a radiant Jeanne, very different from the mournful creature who had accompanied Captain Cranster's victim to Inkston a few weeks before—was sitting up for her mistress and, since she had to perform this duty—which was sweetened by the hope of receiving exciting confidences, for surely that affair was "marching?"—it had been agreed between her and the other maids that she should sit up for the Doctor also. She told the lovers that Doctor Mary had been called for by Mr. Beaumaroy, and had gone out with him, presumably to visit his friend Mr. Saffron. It did not occur to either of them to ask when Mary had set out; they contented themselves with exchanging a glance of disapproval. What a pity that Mary should have anything more to do with this Mr. Saffron and his Beaumaroy!

However there was a bright side to it this time. It would be kind of Cynthia to sit up for Mary, and minister to her a cup of tea which Jeanne should prepare; and it would be pleasant—and quite permissible—for Captain Alec to bear her company. Mary could not be long, surely; it grew late.

So for a while they thought no more of Mary—as was natural enough. They had so much to talk about, the whole of a new and very wonderful life to speculate about and to plan, the whole of their past acquaintance to review; old doubts had to be confessed and laughed at; the inevitability of the whole thing from the first beginnings had to be recognized, proved, and exhibited. In this sweet discourse the minutes flew by unmarked, and would have gone on flying, had not Jeanne reappeared of her own accord, to remark that it really was very late now; did mademoiselle think that possibly anything could have happened to Doctor Arkroyd?

"By Jove, it is late!" cried the Captain, looking at his watch. "It's past one!"

Cynthia was amazed to hear that.

"He must be very ill, that old gentleman," Jeanne opined. "And poor Doctor Arkroyd will be very tired. She will find the walk across the heath very fatiguing."

"Walk, Jeanne? Didn't she take the car?" cried Cynthia, surprised.

No, the Doctor had not taken the car; she had started to walk with Mr. Beaumaroy; the parlormaid had certainly told Jeanne that.

"I tell you what," said the Captain. "I'll just tool along to Tower Cottage. I'll look out for Doctor Mary on the road, and give her a lift back if I meet her. If I don't, I can stop at the cottage and get Beaumaroy to tell her that I'm there, and can wait to bring her home as soon as she's ready. You'd better go to bed, Cynthia."

Jeanne tactfully disappeared, and the lovers said good-night. After Alec's departure, Jeanne received the anticipated confidence.

That departure almost synchronized with two events at Tower Cottage. The first was Beaumaroy's exit from the front door, leaving Mary in charge of his prisoner who, consequently, was unable to keep any watch on the road or to warn his principals of approaching danger. The second was big Neddy's declaration that, in his opinion, the sack now held about as much as he could carry. He raised it from the floor in his two hands. "Must weight a 'undred pound or more!" he reckoned. That meant a lot of money, a fat lot of money. His terrors had begun to wear off, since nothing of a supernatural or even creepy order had actually happened. He had, at last, even agreed to the candles being put out. Still he would be glad to be off. "Enough's as good as a feast, as the sayin' goes, Mike," he chuckled.

Mike had fitted a new battery into his torch. It shone brightly on Neddy and on the sack, whose mouth Neddy was now tying up, "I might fill my pockets too," he suggested, eyeing the very respectable amount of sovereigns which still remained in Captain Duggle's tomb.

"Don't do it, old lad," Neddy advised. "If we 'ave to get out, or anything of that kind, you don't want to jingle as if you was a glass chandelier, do you?"

Mike admitted the cogency of the objection, and they agreed to be off. Mike started for the window. "I'll just pick up the Sergeant," he said, "and signal you 'All clear.' Then you follow out."

"No, Mike," said Neddy slowly, but very decisively. "If you don't mind, it's going to be me as gets out of that window first. I ain't a man of your eddication, and—well, blast me if I'm going to be left in this place alone with—that there!" He motioned with his head, back over his shoulder, towards where silent Mr. Saffron sat.

"You're a blooming ass, Neddy, but have it your own way. Only let me see the coast's clear first."

He stole to the window and looked around. He assumed that the Sergeant was at his post, but all the same he wanted to have a look at the road himself. So he had, and the result was satisfactory. It was hardly to be expected that he should scrutinize the ground immediately under the window; at any rate he did not think of that. It was, as Beaumaroy had conjectured, from another direction, from the parlor, that he anticipated a possible attack. There all was quiet. He came back and reported to Neddy that the moment was favorable. "I'll switch off the torch, though, just in case. You can feel your way; keep to the edge of the steps; don't knock up against—"

"I'll take damned good care not to!" muttered Neddy, with a little shiver.

He made his way to the window, through the darkness, having slung his sack over his shoulder and holding it with his right hand, while with the left he guided himself up the dais and along its outside edge, giving as wide a berth as possible to the great chair and its encircling canopy. With a sigh of relief he found the window, moved the sack from his shoulder, and set it on the ledge for a moment. But it was awkward to get down from the window, holding that heavy sack. He lowered it towards the ground, so that it might land gently, and, just as he let it go, he turned his head back and whispered to Mike, "All serene. Get a move on!"

"Half a minute!" answered Mike, as he in his turn set out to grope his way to the window.

But he was not so cautious as his friend had been. In his progress he kicked the tall footstool sharply with one of his feet. Neddy leant back from the window, asking quickly, and again very nervously, "What the devil's that?"

Beaumaroy could not resist the opportunity thus offered to him. He was crouching on the ground, not exactly under the window, but just to the right of it. Neddy's face was turned away; he threw himself on to the bag, rose to his feet, raised it cautiously, and holding it in front of him with both his hands—its weight was fully as much as he could manage—was round the curve of the Tower and out of sight with it in an instant.

At the back of the house there was a space of ground where Mrs. Wiles grew a few vegetables for the household's use. It was a clearing made from the heath, but it was not enclosed. Beaumaroy was able to reach the back entrance, by which this patch of ground could be entered from the kitchen. Just by the kitchen door stood that useful thing, a butt for rainwater. It stood some three, or three-and-a-half, feet high; and it was full to the brim almost. With a fresh effort Beaumaroy raised the sack to the level of his breast. Then he lowered it into the water, not dropping it, for fear of a splash, but immersing both his arms above the elbow. Only when he felt the weight off them, as the sack touched bottom, did he release his hold. Then with cautious steps he continued his progress round the house and, coming to the other side, crouched close by the wall again and waited. Where he was now, he could see the fence that separated the front garden from the road, and he was not more than ten or twelve feet from the front door on his left. As he huddled down there, he could not repress a smile of amusement, even of self-congratulation. However, he turned to the practical job of squeezing the water out of his sleeves.

In thus congratulating himself, he was premature. His action had been based on a miscalculation. He had heard only Neddy's last exclamation, not the cautious whispers previously exchanged between him and Mike; he thought that the man astride the window-sill himself had kicked something and instinctively exclaimed, "What the devil's that?" He thought that the sack was lowered from the window in order to be committed to the temporary guardianship of the Sergeant, who was doubtless looking out for it and, if he had his ears open, would hear its gentle thud. Perhaps the man in the Tower was collecting a second instalment of booty; heavy as the sack was, it did not contain all that he knew to be in Captain Duggle's grave. Be that as it might, the man would climb out of the window soon; and he would fail to find his sack.

What would he do then? He would signal or call to the Sergeant; or, if they had a preconcerted rendezvous, he would betake himself there, expecting to find his accomplice. He would neither get an answer from him nor find him, of course. Equally, of course, he would look for him. But the last place where he would expect to find him—the last place he would search—would be where the Sergeant in fact was, the house itself. If, in his search for Hooper, he found Beaumaroy, it would be man to man, and, now again, Beaumaroy had no objection.

But, in fact, there were two men in the Tower—one of them big Neddy; and the function, which Beaumaroy supposed to have been intrusted to the Sergeant, had never been assigned to him at all; to guard the door and the road had been his only tasks. When they found the bag gone, and the Sergeant too, they might well think that the Sergeant had betrayed them; that he had gone off on his own account, or that he had, at the last moment, under an impulse of fear or a calculation of interest, changed sides and joined the garrison in the house. If he had gone off with the sack, he could not have gone fast or far with it. Failing to overtake him, they might turn back to the cottage; for they knew themselves to be in superior force. Beaumaroy was in greater danger than he knew—and so was Doctor Mary in the house.

Big Neddy let himself down from the window, and put down his hand to lift up the sack; he groped about for it for some seconds, during which time Mike also climbed over the window-sill and dropped on to the ground below. Neddy emitted a low but strenuous oath.

"The sack's gone, Mike!" he added in a whisper.

"Gone? Rot! Can't be! What do you mean, Neddy?"

"I dropped it straight 'ere. It's gone," Neddy persisted. "The Sergeant must 'ave took it."

"No business of his! Where is the fool?" Mike's voice was already uneasy; thieves themselves seldom believe in there being honor among them. "You stay here. I'll go to the door and see if he's there."

He was just about to put this purpose into execution—in which event it was quite likely that Beaumaroy, hearing his approach or his call to the Sergeant, would have sprung out upon him, only to find himself assailed the next instant by another and far more formidable antagonist in the person of big Neddy, and thus in sore peril of his life—when the hum of Captain Alec's engine became audible in the distance. The next moment, the lights of his car became visible to all the men in the little front garden of the cottage.

"Hist! Wait till that's gone by!" whispered Neddy.

"Yes, and get round to the back. Get out of sight round here." He drew Neddy round the curve of the Tower wall till his big frame was hidden by it; then he himself crouched down under the wall, with his head cautiously protruded. The night had grown clearer; it was possible to see figures at a distance of some yards now.

Beaumaroy also perceived the car. Whose it was and the explanation of its appearance even occurred to his mind. But he kept still. He did not want visitors; he conceived his hand to be a better one than it really was, and preferred to play it by himself. If the car passed by, well and good. Only if it stopped at the gate would he have to take action.

It did stop at the gate. Mike saw it stop. Then its engine was shut off, and a man got out of it, and came up to the garden gate. Though the watching Mike had never seen him before, he had little difficulty in guessing who he was, and he remembered something that the Sergeant had said about him. Of a certainty it was the redoubtable Captain Naylor. Through the darkness he loomed enormous, as tall as big Neddy himself and no whit less broad. A powerful reinforcement for the garrison!

And what would the Sergeant do, if he were still at his post by the door—with or without that missing, that all-important, sack?

Another tall figure came into Mike's view—from where he could not distinctly see; it hardly seemed to be from the door of the cottage, for no light showed, and there was no sound of an opening door. But it appeared from somewhere near there; it was on the path, and it moved along to the gate in a leisurely unhurried approach. A man with his hands in his pockets—that was what it looked like. This must be the garrison; this must be the Sergeant's friend, master, protector, and *bête noire,* his "Boomery."

But the Sergeant himself? Where was he? He could hardly be at his post; or Beaumaroy and he must have seen one another, must have taken some heed of one another; something must have passed between them, either friendly or hostile. Mike turned round and whispered hastily, close into Neddy's ear. Neddy crawled a little forward, and put his own bullet head far enough round the curve of the wall to see the meeting between the garrison and its unexpected reinforcement.

Beaumaroy, hands in pockets, lounged nonchalantly down to the gate. He opened it; the Captain entered. The two shook hands and stood there, apparently in conversation. The words did not reach the ears of the listeners, but the sound of voices did—voices hushed in tone. Once Beaumaroy pointed to the house; both Mike and Neddy marked the outstretched hand. Was Beaumaroy telling his companion about something that had been happening at the house? Were they concocting a plan of defense—or of attack? With the disappearance, perhaps the treachery, of the Sergeant, and the appearance of this new ally for the garrison, the prospects of a fight took on a very different look. Neddy might tackle the big stranger with an equal chance. How would Mike fare in an encounter with Beaumaroy? He did not relish the idea of it.

And, while they fought, the traitor Sergeant might be on their backs! Or—on the other hypothesis—he might be getting off with the swag! Neither alternative was satisfactory.

"P'r'aps he's gone off to the car with the sack—in a fright, like, thinking we'll guess that!" whispered Neddy.

Mike did not much think so, though he would much have liked to. But he received the suggestion kindly. "We might as well have a look; we can come back afterwards if—if we like. Perhaps that big brute'll have gone."

"The thing as I want to do most is to wring that Sergeant's neck!"

Their whispers were checked by a new development. The cottage door opened for a moment and then closed again; they could tell that, both by the sound and by the momentary ray of light. Yet a light persisted after the door was shut. It came from a candle, which burnt steadily in the stillness of the night. It was carried by a woman, who came down the path towards where Beaumaroy and the Captain stood in conversation. Both turned towards her with eager attention.

"Now's our time, then! They aren't looking our way now. We can get across the heath to where the car is."

They moved off very softly, keeping the Tower between them and the group on the path. They gained the back of the house, and so the open heath, and made off to their destination. They moved so softly that they escaped unheard—unless Beaumaroy were right in the notion that his ear caught a little rustle of the bracken. He took no heed of it, unless a passing smile might be reckoned as such.

Doctor Mary joined him and the Captain on the path. Beaumaroy's smile gave way to a look of expectant interest. He wondered what she was going to say to Captain Alec. There was so much that she might say, or—just conceivably—leave unsaid.

She spoke calmly and quietly. "It's you, Captain Alec! I thought so! Cynthia got anxious? I'm all right. I suppose Mr. Beaumaroy has told you? Poor Mr. Saffron is dead."

"I've told him," said Beaumaroy.

"Of heart disease," Mary added. "Quite painlessly, I think—and quite a normal case, though, of course, it's distressing."

"I—I'm sorry," stammered Captain Alec.

Beaumaroy's eyes met Mary's in the candle's light with a swift glance of surprise and inquiry.

Chapter 16

Dead Majesty

Mary did not appear to answer Beaumaroy's glance; she continued to look at, and to address herself to, Captain Alec. "I am tired, and I should love a ride home. But I've still a little to do, and—I know it's awfully late, but would you mind waiting just a little while? I'm afraid I might be as much as half-an-hour."

"Right you are, Doctor Mary—as long as you like. I'll walk up and down, and smoke a cigar; I want one badly." Mary made an extremely faint motion of her hand towards the house. "Oh, thanks, but really I—well, I shall feel more comfortable here, I think."

Mary smiled; it was always safe to rely on Captain Alec's fine feelings; under the circumstances he would— she had felt pretty sure—prefer to smoke his cigar outside the house. "I'll be as quick as I can. Come, Mr. Beaumaroy!"

Beaumaroy followed her up the path and into the house. The Sergeant was still on the floor of the passage; he rolled apprehensive resentful eyes at them; Mary took no heed of him, but preceded Beaumaroy into the parlor and shut the door.

"I don't know what your game is," remarked Beaumaroy in a low voice, "but you couldn't have played mine better. I don't want him inside the house; but I'm mighty glad to have him extremely visible outside it."

"It was very quiet inside there"—she pointed to the door of the Tower—"just before I came out. Before that, I'd heard odd sounds. Was there somebody there—and the Sergeant in league with him?"

"Exactly," smiled Beaumaroy. "It is all quiet. I think I'll have a look."

The candle on the table had burnt out. He took another from the sideboard and lit it from the one which Mary still held.

"Like the poker?" she asked, with a flicker of a smile on her face.

"No you come and help, if I cry out!" He could not repress a chuckle; Doctor Mary was interesting him extremely.

Lighted by his candle, he went into the Tower. She heard him moving about there, as she stood thoughtfully by the extinct fire, still with her candle in her hand.

Beaumaroy returned. "He's gone—or they've gone." He exhibited to her gaze two objects—a checked pocket-handkerchief and a tobacco pouch. "Number one found on the edge of the grave—Number two on the floor of the dais, just behind the canopy. If the same man had drawn them both out of the same pocket at the same time—wanting to blow the same nose, Doctor Mary—they'd have fallen at the same place, wouldn't they?"

"Wonderful, Holmes!" said Mary. "And now, shall we attend to Mr. Saffron?"

They carried out that office, the course of which they had originally prepared. Beaumaroy passed with his burden hard by the Sergeant, and Mary followed. In a quarter of an hour they came downstairs again, and Mary again led the way into the parlor. She went to the window, and drew the curtains aside a little way. The lights of the car were burning; the Captain's tall figure fell within their rays and was plainly visible, strolling up and down; the ambit of the rays did not, however, embrace the Tower window. The Captain paced and smoked, patient, content, gone back to his own happy memories and anticipations. Mary returned to the table and set her candle down on it.

"All right. I think we can keep him a little longer."

"I vote we do," said Beaumaroy. "I reckon he's scared the fellows away, and they won't come back so long as they see his lights."

Rash at conclusions sometimes—as has been seen—Beaumaroy was right in his opinion of the Captain's value as a sentry, or a scarecrow to keep away hungry birds. The confederates had stolen back to their base of operations—to where their car lay behind the trees. There, too, no Sergeant and no sack! Neddy reached for his roomy flask, drank of it, and with hoarse curses consigned the entire course of events, his accomplices, even himself, to nethermost perdition. "That place ain't—natural!" he ended in a gloomy conviction. "'Oo pinched that sack? The Sergeant? Well—maybe it was, and maybe it wasn't." He finished the flask to cure a recurrence of the shudders.

Mike prevailed with him so far that he consented—reluctantly—to be left alone on the blasted heath, while his friend went back to reconnoiter. Mike went, and presently returned; the car was still there, the tall figure was still pacing up and down.

169

"And perhaps the other one's gone for the police!" Mike suggested uneasily. "Guess we've lost the hand, Neddy! Best be moving, eh? It's no go for to-night."

"Catch me trying the bloomin' place any other night!" grumbled Neddy. "It's given me the 'orrors, and no mistake."

Mike—Mr. Percy Bennett, that erstwhile gentlemanly stranger—recognized one of his failures. Such things are incidental to all professions. "Our best game is to go back; if the Sergeant's on the square, we'll hear from him." But he spoke without much hope; rationalist as he professed himself, still he was affected by the atmosphere of the Tower. With what difficulty do we entirely throw off atavistic notions! They both of them had, at the bottom of their minds, the idea that the dead man on the high seat had defeated them, and that no luck lay in meddling with his treasure.

"I 'ave my doubts whether that ugly Sergeant's 'uman himself," growled Neddy, as he hoisted his bulk into the car.

So they went back to whence they came; and the impression that the night's adventure left upon them was heightened as the days went by. For, strange to say, though they watched all the usual channels of information, as Ministers say; in Parliament, and also tried to open up some unusual ones, they never heard anything again of the Sergeant, of the sack of gold, of the yawning tomb with its golden lining, of its silent waxen-faced enthroned guardian who had defeated them. It all—the whole bizarre scene—vanished from their ken, as though it had been one of those alluring, thwarting dreams which afflict men in sleep. It was an experience to which they were shy of alluding among their confidential friends, even of talking about between themselves. In a word—uncomfortable!

Meanwhile the Sergeant's association with Tower Cottage had also drawn to its close. After his search and his discovery in the Tower, Beaumaroy came out into the passage where the prisoner lay, and proceeded to unfasten his bonds.

"Stand up and listen to me, Sergeant," he said. "Your pals have run away; they can't help you, and they wouldn't if they could, because, owing to you, they haven't got away with any plunder, and so they'll be in a very bad temper with you. In the road, in front of the house, is Captain Naylor—you know that officer and his dimensions? He's in a very temper with you too. (Here Beaumaroy was embroidering the situation; the Sergeant was not really in Captain Alec's thoughts.) Finally, I'm in a very bad temper with you myself. If I see your ugly phiz much longer, I may break out. Don't you think you'd better depart—by the back door—and go home? And if you're not out of Inkston for good and all by ten o'clock in the morning, and if you ever show yourself there again, look out for squalls. What you've got out of this business I don't know. You can keep it—and I'll give you a parting present myself as well."

"I knows a thing or two—" the Sergeant began, but he saw a look that he had seen only once or twice before on Beaumaroy's face; on each occasion it had been followed by the death of the enemy whose act had elicited it.

"Oh, try that game, just try it!" Beaumaroy muttered. "Just give me that excuse!" He advanced to the Sergeant, who fell suddenly on his knees. "Don't make a noise, you hound, or I'll silence you for good and all—I'd do it for twopence!" He took hold of the Sergeant's coat-collar, jerked him on to his legs, and propelled him to the kitchen and through it to the back door. Opening it, he dispatched the Sergeant through the doorway with an accurate and vigorous kick. He fell, and lay sprawling on the ground for a second, then gathered himself up and ran hastily over the heath, soon disappearing in the darkness. The memory of Beaumaroy's look was even keener than the sensation caused by Beaumaroy's boot. It sent him in flight back to Inkston, thence to London, thence into the unknown, to some spot chosen for its remoteness from Beaumaroy, from Captain Naylor, from Mike and from Neddy. He recognized his unpopularity, thereby achieving a triumph in a difficult little branch of wisdom.

Beaumaroy returned to the parlor hastily; not so much to avoid keeping Captain Alec waiting—it was quite a useful precaution to have that sentry on duty a little longer—as because his curiosity and interest had been excited by the description which Doctor Mary had given of Mr. Saffron's death. It was true, probably the precise truth, but it seemed to have been volunteered in a rather remarkable way and worded with careful purpose. Also it was the bare truth, the truth denuded of all its attendant circumstances—which had not been normal.

When he rejoined her, Mary was sitting in the armchair by the fire; she heard his account of the state of affairs up-to-date with a thoughtful smile, smoking a cigarette; her smile broadened over the tale of the water-butt. She had put on the fur cloak in which she had walked to the cottage—the fire was out and the room cold; framed in the furs, the outline of her face looked softer.

"So we stand more or less as we did before the burglars appeared on the scene," she commented.

"Except that our personal exertions have saved that money."

"I suppose you would prefer that all the circumstances shouldn't come out? There have been irregularities."

"I should prefer that, not so much on my own account—I don't know and don't care what they could do to me—as for the old man's sake."

"If I know you, I think you would rather enjoy being able to keep your secret. You like having the laugh of people. I know that myself, Mr. Beaumaroy." She exchanged a smile with him. "You want a death certificate from me," she added.

"I suppose I do," Beaumaroy agreed.

"In the sort of terms in which I described Mr. Saffron's death to Captain Alec? If I gave such a certificate, there would remain nothing—well, nothing peculiar—except the—the appearance of things in the Tower."

Her eyes were now fixed on his face; he nodded his head with a smile of understanding. There was something new in the tone of Doctor Mary's voice; not only friendliness, though that was there, but a note of excitement, of enjoyment, as though she also were not superior to the pleasure of having the laugh of people. "But it's rather straining a point to say that—and nothing more. I could do it only if you made me feel that I could trust you absolutely."

Beaumaroy made a little grimace, and waited for her to develop her subject.

"Your morality is different from most people's, and from mine. Mine is conventional."

"Conventual!" Beaumaroy murmured.

"Yours isn't. It's all personal with you. You recognize no rights in people whom you don't like, or who you think aren't deserving, or haven't earned rights. And you don't judge your own rights by what the law gives you, either. The right of conquest you called it; you hold yourself free to exercise that against everybody, except your friends, and against everybody in the interest of your friends—like poor Mr. Saffron. I believe you'd do the same for me if I asked you to."

"I'm glad you believe that, Doctor Mary."

"But I can't deal with you on that basis. It's even difficult to be friends on that basis—and certainly impossible to be partners."

"I never suggested that we should be partners over the money," Beaumaroy put in quickly.

"No. But I'm suggesting now—as you did before—that we should be partners—in a secret, in Mr. Saffron's secret." She smiled again as she added, "You can manage it all, I know, if you like. I've unlimited confidence in your ingenuity—quite unlimited."

"But none at all in my honesty?"

"You've got an honesty; but I don't call it a really honest honesty."

"All this leads up to—the Radbolts!" declared Beaumaroy with &gesture of disgust.

"It does. I want your word of honor—given to a friend— that all that money—all of it—goes to the Radbolts, if it legally belongs to them. I want that in exchange for the certificate."

"A hard bargain! It isn't so much that I want the money—though I must remark that in my judgment I have a strong claim to it; I would say a moral claim but for my deference to your views, Doctor Mary. But it isn't mainly that. I hate the Radbolts getting it, just as much as the old man would have hated it."

"I have given you my—my terms," said Mary.

Beaumaroy stood looking down at her, his hands in his pockets. His face was twisted in a humorous disgust. Mary laughed gently. "It is possible to—to keep the rules without being a prig, you know, though I believe you think it isn't."

"Including the sack in the water-butt? My sack, the sack I rescued?"

"Including the sack in the water-butt. Yes, every single sovereign!" Though Mary was pursuing the high moral line, there was now more mischief than gravity in her demeanor.

"Well, I'll do it!" He evidently spoke with a great effort. "I'll do it! But, look here, Doctor Mary, you'll live to be sorry you made me do it. Oh, I don't mean that that conscience of yours will be sorry. That'll approve, no doubt, being the extremely conventionalized thing it is. But you yourself, you'll be sorry, or I'm much mistaken in the Radbolts."

"It isn't a question of the Radbolts," she insisted, laughing.

"Oh yes, it is, and you'll come to feel it so." Beaumaroy was equally obstinate.

Mary rose. "Then that's settled, and we needn't keep Captain Alec waiting any longer."

"How do you know that I sha'n't cheat you?" he asked.

"I don't know how I know that," Mary admitted. "But I do know it. And I want to tell you—"

She suddenly felt embarrassed under his gaze; her cheeks flushed, but she went on resolutely:

"To tell you how glad, how happy, I am that it all ends like this; that the poor old man is free of his fancies and his fears, beyond both our pity and our laughter."

"Aye, he's earned rest, if there is to be rest for any of us!"

"And you can rest, too. And you can laugh with us, and not at us. Isn't that, after all, a more human sort of laughter?"

She was smiling still as she gave him her hand, but he saw that tears stood in her eyes. The next instant she gave a little sob.

"Doctor Mary!" he exclaimed in rueful expostulation.

"No, no, how stupid you are!" She laughed through her sob. "It's not unhappiness!" She pressed his hand tightly for an instant and then walked quickly out of the house, calling back to him, "Don't come, please don't come. I'd rather go to Captain Alec by myself."

Left alone in the cottage, now so quiet and so peaceful, Beaumaroy mused a while as he smoked his pipe. Then he turned to his labors—his final night of work in the Tower. There was much to do, very much to do; he achieved his task towards morning. When day dawned, there was nothing but water in the water-butt, and in the Tower no furnishings were visible save three chairs—a high carved one by the fireplace, and two much smaller on the little platform under the window. The faded old red carpet on the floor was the only attempt at decoration. And in still one thing more the Tower was different from what it had been, Beaumaroy contented himself with pasting brown paper over the pane on which Mike had operated. He did not replace the matchboarding over the window, but stowed it away in the coal-shed. The place was horribly in need of sunshine and fresh air—and the old gentleman was no longer alive to fear the draught!

When the undertaker came up to the cottage that afternoon, he glanced from the parlor, through the open door, into the Tower.

"Driving past on business, sir," he remarked to Beaumaroy, "I've often wondered what the old gentleman did with that there Tower. But it looks as if he didn't make no use of it."

"We sometimes stored things in it," said Beaumaroy. "But, as you see, there's nothing much there now."

But then the undertaker, worthy man, could not see through the carpet, or through the lid of Captain Duggle's grave. That was full—fuller than it had been at any period of its history. In it lay the wealth, the scepter, and the trappings of dead Majesty. For wherein did Mr. Saffron's dead Majesty differ from the dead Majesty of other Kings?

Chapter 17

The Chief Mourners

The attendance was small at Mr. Saffron's funeral. Besides meek and depressed Mrs. Wiles, and Beaumaroy himself, Doctor Mary found herself, rather to her surprise, in company with old Mr. Naylor. On comparing notes she discovered that, like herself, he had come on Beaumaroy's urgent invitation and, moreover, that he was engaged also to come on afterwards to Tower Cottage, where Beaumaroy was to entertain the chief mourners at a mid-day repast. "Glad enough to show my respect to a neighbor," said old Naylor. "And I always liked the old man's looks. But really I don't see why I should go to lunch. However, Beaumaroy—"

Mary did not see why he should go to lunch—nor, for that matter, why she should either, but curiosity about the chief mourners made her glad that she was going. The chief mourners did not look, at first sight, attractive. Mr. Radbolt was a short plump man, with a weaselly face and cunning eyes; his wife's eyes, of a greeny color, stared stolidly out from her broad red face; she was taller than her mate, and her figure contrived to be at once stout and angular. All through the service, Beaumaroy's gaze was set on the pair as they sat or stood in front of him, wandering from the one to the other in an apparently fascinated study.

At the Cottage he entertained his party in the parlor with a generous hospitality, and treated the Radbolts with most courteous deference. The man responded with the best manners that he had—who can do more? The woman was much less cordial; she was curt, and treated Beaumaroy rather as the servant than the friend of her dead cousin; there was a clear suggestion of suspicion in her bearing towards him. After a broad stare of astonishment on her introduction to "Dr. Arkroyd," she took very little notice of Mary; only to Mr. Naylor was she clumsily civil and even rather cringing; it was clear that in him she acknowledged the gentleman. He sat by her, and she tried to insinuate herself into a private conversation with him, apart from the others, probing him as to his knowledge of the dead man and his mode of living. Her questions hovered persistently round the point of Mr. Saffron's expenditure.

"Mr. Saffron was not a friend of mine," Naylor found it necessary to explain. "I had few opportunities of observing his way of life, even if I had felt any wish to do so."

"I suppose Beaumaroy knew all about his affairs," she suggested.

"As to that, I think you must ask Mr. Beaumaroy himself."

"From what the lawyers say, the old man seems to have been getting rid of his money, somehow or to somebody," she grumbled, in a positive whisper.

To Mr. Naylor's intense relief, Beaumaroy interrupted this conversation. "Well, how do you like this little place,

Mrs. Radbolt?" he asked cheerfully. "Not a bad little crib, is it? Don't you think so too, Dr. Arkroyd?" Throughout this gathering Beaumaroy was very punctilious with his "Dr. Arkroyd." One would have thought that Mary and he were almost strangers.

"Yes, I like it," said Mary. "The Tower makes it rather unusual and picturesque." This was not really her sincere opinion; she was playing up to Beaumaroy, convinced that he had opened some conversational maneuver.

"Don't like it at all," answered Mrs. Radbolt. "We'll get rid of it as soon as we can, won't we, Radbolt?" She always addressed her husband as "Radbolt."

"Don't be in a hurry, don't throw it away," Beaumaroy advised. "It's not everybody's choice, of course, but there are quarters—yes, more than one quarter—in which you might get a very good offer for this place." His eye caught Mary's for a moment. "Indeed I wish I was in a position to make you one myself. I should like to take it as it stands—lock, stock and barrel. But I've sunk all I had in another venture—hope it turns out a satisfactory one! So I'm not in a position to do it. If Mrs. Radbolt wants to sell, what would you think of it, Dr. Arkroyd, as a speculation?"

Mary shook her head, smiling, glad to be able to smile with plausible reason. "I'm not as fond of rash speculations as you are, Mr. Beaumaroy."

"It may be worth more than it looks," he pursued. "Good neighborhood, healthy air, fruitful soil, very rich soil hereabouts."

"My dear Beaumaroy, the land about here is abominable," Naylor expostulated.

"Perhaps generally, but some rich pockets—one may call pockets," corrected Beaumaroy.

"I'm not an agriculturist," remarked weaselly Mr. Radbolt, in his oily tones.

"And then there's a picturesque old yarn told about it—oh, whether it's true or not, of course I don't know. It's about a certain Captain Duggle—not the Army—the Mercantile Marine, Mrs. Radbolt. You know the story Dr. Arkroyd? And you too, Mr. Naylor? You're the oldest inhabitant of Inkston present, sir. Suppose you tell it to Mr. and Mrs. Radbolt? I'm sure it will make them attach a new value to this really very attractive cottage—with, as Dr. Arkroyd says, the additional feature of the Tower."

"I know the story only as a friend of mine—Mr. Penrose—who takes great interest in local records and traditions, told it to me. If our host desires, I shall be happy to tell it to Mrs. Radbolt." Mr. Naylor accompanied his words with a courtly little bow to that lady, and launched upon the legend of Captain Duggle.

Mr. Radbolt was a religious man. At the end of the story he observed gravely, "The belief in diabolical personalities is not to be lightly dismissed, Mr. Beaumaroy."

"I'm entirely of your opinion, Mr. Radbolt." This time Mary felt that her smile was not so plausible.

"There seems to have been nothing in the grave," mused Mrs. Radbolt.

"Apparently not when Captain Duggle left it—if he was ever in it—at all events not when he left the house, in whatever way and by whatever agency."

"As to the latter point, I myself incline to Penrose's theory," said Mr. Naylor. "*Delirium tremens,* you know!"

Beaumaroy puffed at his cigar. "Still, I've often thought that, though it was empty then, it would have made—supposing it really exists—an excellent hiding-place for anybody who wanted such a thing. Say, for a miser, or a man who had his reasons for concealing what he was worth! I once suggested the idea to Mr. Saffron, and he was a good deal amused. He patted me on the shoulder and laughed heartily. He wasn't often so much amused as that."

A new look came into Mrs. Radbolt's green eyes. Up to now, distrust of Beaumaroy had predominated. His frank bearing, his obvious candor and simplicity, had weakened her suspicions. But his words suggested something else; he might be a fool, not a knave; Mr. Saffron had been amused, had laughed beyond his wont. That might have seemed the best way of putting Beaumaroy off the scent. The green eyes were now alert, eager, immensely acquisitive.

"The grave's in the Tower, if it's anywhere. Would you like to see the Tower, Mrs. Radbolt?"

"Yes, I should," she answered tartly. "Being part of our property as it is."

Mary exchanged a glance with Mr. Naylor, as they followed the others into the Tower. "What an abominable woman!" her glance said. Naylor smiled a despairing acquiescence.

The strangers—chief mourners, heirs-at-law, owners now of the place wherein they stood—looked round the bare brick walls of the little rotunda. Naylor examined it with interest too—the old story was a quaint one. Mary stood at the back of the group, smiling triumphantly. How had he disposed of—everything? She had not been wrong in her unlimited confidence in his ingenuity. She did not falter in her faith in his word pledged to her.

"Safe from burglars, that grave of the Captain's, if you kept it properly concealed!" Beaumaroy pursued in a sort of humorous meditation. "And in these days some people like to have their money in their own hands. Confiscatory legislation possible, isn't it, Mr. Naylor? You know about those things better than I do. And then the taxes—shocking, Mr. Radbolt! By Jove, I knew a chap the other day who came in for what sounded like a pretty little inheritance. But by the time he'd paid all the duties and so on, most of the gilt was off the gingerbread! It's there—in front of the hearth—that the story says the grave is. Doesn't it, Mr. Naylor?" A sudden thought seemed to strike him, "I say, Mrs. Radbolt, would you like us to have a look whether we can find any indications of it?" His eyes traveled beyond the lady whom he addressed. They met Mary's. She knew their message; he was taking her into his confidence about his experiment with the chief mourners.

The stout angular woman had leapt to her conclusion. Much less money than had been expected—no signs of money having been spent and here, not the cunning knave whom she had expected, but a garrulous open fool, giving away what was perhaps a golden secret! Mammon, the greed of acquisitiveness, the voracious appetite for getting more, gleamed in her green eyes.

"There? Do you say it's—it's supposed to be there?" she asked eagerly, with a shake in her voice.

Her husband interposed in a suave and sanctimonious voice: "My dear, if Mr. Beaumaroy and the other gentleman won't mind my saying so, I've been feeling that these are rather light and frivolous topics for the day, and the occasion which brings us here. The whole thing is probably an unfounded story, although there is a sound moral to it. Later on, just as a matter of curiosity, if you like, my dear. But to-day, Cousin Aloysius's day of burial, is it quite seemly?"

The big woman looked at her smaller mate for just a moment, a scrutinizing look. Then she said with most un-expected meekness, "I was wrong. You always have the proper feelings, Radbolt."

"The fault was mine, entirely mine," Beaumaroy hastily interposed. "I dragged in the old yarn, I led Mr. Naylor into telling it, I told you about what I said to Mr. Saffron and how he took it. All my fault! I acknowledge the jus-tice of your rebuke. I apologize, Mr. Radbolt! And I think that we've exhausted the interest of the Tower." He looked at his watch. "Er, how do you stand for time? Shall Mrs. Wiles make us a cup of tea, or have you a train to catch?"

"That's the woman in charge of the house, isn't it?" asked Mrs. Radbolt.

"Comes in for the day. She doesn't sleep here." He smiled pleasantly on Mrs. Radbolt. "To tell you the truth, I don't think that she would consent to sleep here by herself. Silly! But—the old story, you know!"

"Don't you sleep here?" the woman persisted, though her husband was looking at her rather uneasily.

"Up to now I have," said Beaumaroy. "But there's noth-ing to keep me here now, and Mr. Naylor has kindly of-fered to put me up as long as I stay at Inkston."

"Going to leave the place with nobody in it?"

Beaumaroy's manner indicated surprise. "Oh, yes! There's nothing to tempt thieves, is there? Just lock the door and put the key in my pocket!"

The woman looked very surly, but flummoxed. Her hus-band, with his suave oiliness, came to her rescue. "My wife is always nervous, perhaps foolishly nervous, about fire, Mr. Beaumaroy. Well, with an old house like this, there is always the risk."

"Upon my soul, I hadn't thought of it! And I've packed up all my things, and your car's come and fetched them, Mr. Naylor. Still, of course I could—"

"Oh, we've no right, no claim, to trouble you, Mr. Beaumaroy. Only my wife is—"

"Fire's an obsession with me, I'm afraid," said the stout woman, with a rumbling giggle. The sound of her mirth was intolerably disagreeable to Mary.

"I really think, my dear, that you'll feel easier if I stay myself, won't you? You can send me what I want tomorrow, and rejoin me when we arrange—because we shall have to settle what's to be done with the place."

"As you please, Mr. Radbolt." Beaumaroy's tone was, for the first time, a little curt. It hinted some slight offense— as though he felt himself charged with carelessness, and considered Mrs. Radbolt's obsession mere fussiness. "No doubt, if you stay, Mrs. Wiles will agree to stay too, and do her best to make you comfortable."

"I shall feel easier that way, Radbolt," Mrs. Radbolt admitted, with another rumble of apologetic mirth.

Beaumaroy motioned his guests back to the parlor. His manner retained its shade of distance and offense. "Then it really only remains for me to wish you good-bye—and all happiness in your new property. Any information in my possession as to Mr. Saffron's affairs I shall, of course, be happy to give you. Is the car coming for you, Mr. Naylor?"

"I thought it would be pleasant to walk back; and I hope Doctor Mary will come with us and have some tea. I'll send you home afterwards, Doctor Mary."

Farewells were exchanged, but now without even a show of cordiality. Naylor and Doctor Mary felt too much distaste for the chief mourners to attain more than a cold civility. Beaumaroy did not relax into his earlier friendliness. His apparent dislike to her husband's plan of staying at the Cottage roused Mrs. Radbolt's suspicions again; was he a rogue after all, but a very plausible, a very deep one? Only Mr. Radbolt's unctuousness—surely it would have smoothed the stormiest waves—saved the social situation.

"Intelligent people, I thought," Beaumaroy observed, as the three friends pursued their way across the heath towards Old Place. "Didn't you, Mr. Naylor?"

Old Naylor grunted. With a twinkle in his eyes, Beaumaroy tried Doctor Mary. "What was your impression of them?"

"Oh!" moaned Mary, with a deep and expressive note. "But how did you know they'd be like that?"

"Letters, and the old man's description, he had a considerable command of language, and very violent likes and dislikes. I made a picture of them—and it's turned out pretty accurate."

"And those were the nearest kith and kin your poor old man had?" Naylor shook his head sadly. "The woman obviously cared not a straw about anything but handling his money—and couldn't even hide it! A gross and horrible female, Beaumaroy!"

"Were you really hurt about their insisting on staying?" asked Mary.

"Oh, come, you're sharper than that, Doctor Mary! Still, I think I did it pretty well. I set the old girl thinking again, didn't I?" He broke into laughter, and Mary joined in heartily. Old Naylor glanced from one to the other with an air of curiosity.

"You two people look to me—somehow—as if you'd got a secret between you."

"Perhaps we have! Mr. Naylor's a man of honor, Doctor Mary; a man who appreciates a situation, a man you can trust." Beaumaroy seemed very gay and happy now, disembarrassed of a load, and buoyant alike in walk and in spirit. "What do you say to letting Mr. Naylor—just him—nobody else—into our secret?"

Mary put her arms through old Mr. Naylor's. "I don't mind, if you don't. But nobody else!"

"Then you shall tell him—the entire story—at your leisure. Meanwhile I'll begin at the wrong end. I told you I'd made a picture of the hated cousins, of the heirs-at-law, those sorrowing chief mourners. Well, having made a picture of them that's proved true, I'll make a prophecy about them, and I'll bet you it proves just as true."

"Go on," said Mary. "Listen, Mr. Naylor," she added with a squeeze of the old man's arm.

"You're like a couple of naughty children!" he said, with an affectionate look and laugh.

"Well, my prophecy is that they'll swear the poor dear old man's estate at under five thousand."

"Well, why shouldn't—" old Naylor began; but he stopped as he saw Mary's eyes meet Beaumaroy's in a rapture of quick and delighted understanding.

"And then perhaps you'll own to being sorry, Doctor Mary!"

"So that's what you were up to, was it?" said Mary.

Chapter 18

The Gold and the Treasure

Old Mr. Naylor called on Mary two or three days later—at an hour when, as he well knew, Cynthia was at his own house—in order to hear the story. There were parts of it which she could not describe fully for lack of knowledge—the enterprise of Mike and Big Neddy, for example; but all that she knew she told frankly, and did not scruple to invoke her imagination to paint Beaumaroy's position, with its difficulties, demands, obligations—and temptations. He heard her with close attention, evidently amused, and watching her animated face with a keen and watchful pleasure.

"Surprising!" he said at the end, rubbing his hands together. "That's to say, not in itself particularly surprising. Just a queer little happening; one would think nothing of it if one read it in the newspaper! Things are always so much more surprising when they happen down one's own street, or within a few minutes' walk of one's garden wall—and when one actually knows the people involved in them. Still I was always inclined to agree with Dr. Irechester that there was something out of the common about old Saffron and our friend Beaumaroy."

"Dr. Irechester never found out what it was, though!" exclaimed Mary triumphantly.

"No, he didn't; for reasons pretty clearly indicated in your narrative." He sat back in his chair, his elbows on the arms and his hands clasped before him. "If I may say so, the really curious thing is to find you in the thick of it, Doctor Mary."

"That wasn't my fault. I couldn't refuse to attend Mr. Saffron. Dr. Irechester himself said so."

He paid no heed to her protest. "In the thick of it—and enjoying it so tremendously!"

Mary looked thoughtful. "I didn't at first. I was angry, indignant, suspicious. I thought I was being made a fool of."

"So you were—a fool and a tool, my dear!"

"But that night—because it all really happened in just one night—the chief mourners, as Mr. Beaumaroy always calls them, were more than—"

"Just a rather amusing epilogue—yes, that's all."

"That night, it did get hold of me." She laughed a little nervously, a little uneasily.

"And now you tell it to me—I must say that your telling made it twice the story that it really is—now you tell it as if it were the greatest thing that ever happened to you!"

For a moment Mary fenced. "Well, nothing interesting ever has happened in my humdrum life before." But old Naylor pursed up his lips in contempt of her fencing. "It did seem to me a great—a great experience. Not the burglars and all that—though some of the things, like the water-butt, did amuse me very much—but our being apart from all the world, there by ourselves, against the whole world in a way, Mr. Naylor."

"The law on one side, the robbers on the other, and you two alone together!"

"Yes, you understand. That was the way I felt it. But we weren't together, not in every way. I mean, we were fighting between ourselves too, right up to the very end." She gave another low laugh. "I suppose we're fighting still; he means to face me with some Radbolt villainy, and make me sorry for what he calls my legalism—with an epithet!"

"That's his idea, and my own too, I confess. Those chief mourners will find the money—and some other things that'll make 'em stare. But they'll lie low; they'll sit on the cash till the time comes when it's safe to dispose of it; and they'll bilk the Inland Revenue out of the duties. The remarkable thing is that Beaumaroy seems to want them to do it."

"That's to make me sorry; that's to prove me wrong, Mr. Naylor."

"It may make you sorry, it makes me sorry, for that matter; but it doesn't prove you wrong. You were right. My boy Alec would have taken the same line as you did. Now you needn't laugh at me, Mary. I own up at once; that's my highest praise."

"I know it is; and it implies a contrast?"

Old Naylor unclasped his hands and spread them in a deprecatory gesture. "It must do that," he acknowledged.

Mary gave a rebellious little toss of her head. "I don't care if it does, Mr. Naylor! Mr. Beaumaroy is my friend now."

"And mine. Moreover I have such confidence in his honor and fidelity that I have offered him a rather important and confidential position in my business—to represent us at one of the foreign ports where we have considerable interests." He smiled. "It's the sort of place where he will perhaps find himself less trammelled by—er—legalism, and with more opportunities for his undoubted gift of initiative."

"Will he accept your offer? Will he go?" she asked rather excitedly.

"Without doubt, I think. It's really quite a good offer. And what prospects has he now, or here?"

Mary stretched her hands towards the fire and gazed into it in silence.

"I think you'll have an offer soon too, and a good one, Doctor Mary. Irechester was over at our place yesterday. He's still of opinion that there was something queer at Tower Cottage. Indeed he thinks that Mr. Saffron was queer himself, in his head, and that a clever doctor would have found it out."

"That he himself would, if he'd gone on attending—"

"Precisely. But he's not surprised that you didn't; you lacked the experience. Still he thinks none the worse of you for that, and he told me that he has made up his mind to offer you partnership. Irechester's a bit stiff, but a very straight fellow. You could rely on being fairly treated, and it's a good practice. Besides he's well off, and quite likely to retire as soon as he sees you fairly in the saddle."

"It's a great compliment." Here Mary's voice sounded quite straightforward and sincere. An odd little note of contempt crept into it as she added, "And it sounds—ideal!"

"Yes, it does," old Naylor agreed, with a private smile all to himself, whilst Mary still gazed into the fire. "Quite ideal. You're a lucky young woman, Mary." He rose to take his leave. "So, with our young folk happily married, and you installed, and friend Beaumaroy suited to his liking—why, upon my word, we may ring the curtain down on a happy ending—of Act I, at all events!"

She seemed to pay no heed to his words. He stood for a moment, admiring her; not as a beauty, but a healthy comely young woman, stout-hearted, and with humanity and a sense of fun in her. And, as he looked, his true feeling about the situation suddenly burst through all restraint and leapt from his lips. "Though, for my part, under the circumstances, if I were you, I'd see old Irechester damned before I accepted the partnership!"

She turned to him—startled, yet suddenly smiling. He took her hand and raised it to his lips.

"Hush! Not another word! Good-bye, my dear Mary!"

The next day, as Mary, her morning round finished, sat at lunch with Cynthia, listening, or not listening, to her friend's excusably, eager chatter about her approaching wedding, a note was delivered into her hands:

The C.M.'s are in a hurry! She's back! The window is boarded up again! Come and see! About 4 o'clock this afternoon. B.

Mary kept the appointment. She found Beaumaroy strolling up and down on the road in front of the cottage. The Tower window was boarded up again, but with new strong planks, in a much more solid and workmanlike fashion. If he were to try again, Mike would not find it so easy to negotiate, without making a dangerous noise over the job.

"Such impatience—such undisguised rapacity—is indecent and revolting," Beaumaroy remarked. He seemed to be in the highest spirits. "I wonder if they've opened it yet!"

"They'll see you prowling about outside, won't they?"

"I hope so. Indeed I've no doubt of it. Mrs. Greeneyes is probably peering through the parlor window at this minute, and cursing me. I like it! To those people I represent law and order. If they can rise to the conception of such a thing at all, I probably embody conscience. When you come to think of it, it's a pleasant turn of events that I should come to represent law and order and conscience to anybody, even to the Radbolts."

"It is rather a change," she agreed. "But let's walk on. I don't really much want to think of them."

"That's because you feel that you're losing the bet. I can't stop them getting the money in the end, that's your doing! I can't stop them cheating the Revenue, which is what they certainly mean to do, without exposing myself to more inconvenience than I am disposed to undergo in the cause of the Revenue. Whereas if I had left the bag in the water-butt—all your doing! Aren't you a little sorry?"

"Of course there is an aspect of the case—" she admitted smiling.

"That's enough for me! You've lost the bet. Let's see—what were the stakes, Mary?"

"Come, let's walk on." She put her arm through his. "What about this berth that Mr. Naylor's offering you? At Bogota, isn't it?"

He looked puzzled for a moment; then his mind worked quickly back to Cynthia's almost forgotten tragedy. He laughed in enjoyment of her thrust. "My place isn't Bogota—though I fancy that it's rather in the same moral latitude. You're confusing me with Captain Cranster!"

"So I was—for a moment," said Doctor Mary demurely. "But what about the appointment, anyhow?"

"What about your partnership with Dr. Irechester, if you come to that?"

Mary pressed his arm gently, and they walked on in silence for a little while. They were clear of the neighborhood of Tower Cottage now, but still a considerable distance from Old Place; very much alone together on the heath, as they had seemed to be that night—that night of nights—at the cottage.

"I haven't so much as received the offer yet; only Mr. Naylor has mentioned it to me."

"Still, you'd like to be ready with your answer when the offer is made, wouldn't you?" He drew suddenly away from her, and stood still on the road, opposite to her. His face lost its playfulness; as it set into gravity, the lines upon it deepened, and his eyes looked rather sad. "This is wrong of me, perhaps, but I can't help it. I'm not going to talk to you about myself. Confessions and apologies and excuses, and so on, aren't in my line. I should probably tell lies if I attempted anything of the sort. You must take me or leave me on your own judgment, on your own feelings about me, as you've seen and known me—not long, but pretty intimately, Mary." He suddenly reached his hand into his pocket and pulled out the combination knife-and-fork. "That's all I've brought away of his from Tower Cottage. And I brought it away as much for your sake as for his. It was during our encounter over this instrument that I first thought of you as a woman, Mary. And, by Jove, I believe you knew it!"

"Yes, I believe I did," she answered, her eyes set very steadily on his.

He slipped the thing back into his pocket. "And now I love you, and I want you, Mary."

She fell into a sudden agitation. "Oh, but this doesn't seem for me! I'd put all that behind me! I—" She could scarcely find words. "I, I'm just Doctor Mary!"

"Lots of people to practice on—bodies and souls too, in the moral latitude I'm going to!"

Her body seemed to shiver a little, as though before a plunge into deep water. "I'm very safe here," she whispered.

"Yes, you're safe here," he acknowledged gravely, and stood silent, waiting for her choice.

"What a decision to have to make!" she cried suddenly. "It's all my life in a moment! Because I don't want you to go away from me!" She drew near to him, and put her hands on his shoulders. "I'm not a child, like Cynthia. I can't dream dreams and make idols any more. I think I see you as you are, and I don't know whether your love is a good thing." She paused, searching his eyes with hers very earnestly. Then she went on, "But if it isn't, I think there's no good thing left for me at all."

"Mary, isn't that your answer to me?" "Yes." Her arms fell from his shoulders, and she stood opposite to him, in silence again for a moment. Then her troubled face cleared to a calm serenity. "And now I set doubts and fears behind me. I come to you in faith, and loyalty, and love. I'm not a missionary to you, or a reformer, God forbid! I'm just the woman who loves you, Hector."

"I should have mocked at the missionary, and tricked the reformer." He bared his head before her. "But by the woman who loves me and whom I love, I will deal faithfully." He bent and kissed her forehead.

"And now, let's walk on. No, not to old Place—back home, past Tower Cottage."

She put her arm through his again, and they set out through the soft dusk that had begun to hover about them. So they came to the cottage, and here, for a while, instinctively stayed their steps. A light shone in the parlor window; the Tower was dark and still. Mary turned her face to Beaumaroy's with a sudden smile of scornful gladness.

"Aye, aye, you're right!" His smile answered hers. "Poor devils! I'm sorry; for them, upon my soul I am!"

"That really is just like you!" she exclaimed in mirthful exasperation. "Sorry for the Radbolts now, are you?"

"Well, after all, they've only got the gold. We've got the treasure, Mary!"

www.ingramcontent.com/pod-product-compliance
Lightning Source LLC
Chambersburg PA
CBHW020632180626
46816CB00003B/920